including his hypothesis that the Dogon people of Mali preserved an initiatory religious tradition involving contact with intelligent extraterrestrials from the Sirius star system. Robert also offers a piece of his surrealistic fiction, never before published, what he has termed neo-surrealistic. In a similar vein, horror legend Ramsey Campbell—whose novels have influenced so many of us over the years—presents us with a brand new neo-surrealistic story.

Additionally, it is my honor to present a new story from award-winning author Tananarive Due exploring the experience of The Extraterrestrial as "the Other." Up-and-comer Philip Fracassi offers an interesting tale of insectoid aliens, while veteran weird fictionist Jeffrey Thomas takes us back to Punktown for a wild ride. Rjurik Davidson (Caeli-Amur), Sylvain Neuvel (The Themis Files), and Peter Tieryas (United States of Japan) all contribute their fictional perspectives on the theme of The Extraterrestrial. You won't want to miss this. As for non-fiction, Brett Talley delineates the Ancient Alien Theory, and Donald Tyson delivers his astute analysis and summation of Carl Jung's work on UFOs, plus two new film reviews from Colleen Wanglund. A lot to dig into!

Again, I want to thank you for supporting the magazine. I truly appreciate it.

And now—prepare for Contact!

—Aaron J. French
Editor-in-Chief

# *Thursday Night Shift*

BY TANANARIVE DUE

**Publisher**
JournalStone Publishing, LLC

**Editor-in-Chief and Art Director**
Aaron J. French

**Layout and Design**
Jess Landry

**Founding Publisher and Editor**
James R. Beach

**Special Thanks**
Tananarive Due, Robert K.G. Temple, John Coyne, Ramsey Campbell, and Jess Landry

**Contributing Artists**
Steve Santiago (Cover Design)

DARK DISCOVERIES
(ISSN 1548-6842) is published (qrtly) by
JournalStone Publications
3205 Sassafras Trail, Carbondale, IL 62901

**JOURNALSTONE**
YOUR LINK TO ARTISTIC TALENT

# FICTION

# NON-FICTION

# EDITORIAL

Greetings, folks. Welcome to issue #38 of *Dark Discoveries*. As some may have heard, unfortunately due to problems in the print magazine market, i.e. low sales for print mags overall, we are not able to continue to support publishing the magazine *Dark Discoveries* as we have been publishing it. So, we are going to publish this final issue, after which the magazine will be going on an extended hiatus while we regroup and rethink the magazine and determine where to go next with it. I want to thank everyone for their support over the last few years, and all the folks who have contributed, subscribed, and helped me out. I truly appreciate it. I have been learning a lot. Thank you!

I promise this issue will still bring you all the wonderful content and fiction you have come to expect from DD. I want to thank each and every one of you for reading and supporting both myself and the magazine. I also want to give a major thanks to everyone who has assisted me with the magazine and its production over the years, way too many to mention! But a huge thanks to Paul Fry of SST Publications who delivered some amazing interior design work, and also the artists, columnists, reviewers, etc. THANK YOU!

So now, on we go with issue #38. The theme this time is The Extraterrestrial. We've got some wonderful fiction and articles packed into this one. In this issue you'll find a brand new interview with Robert K. G. Temple, internationally known researcher and author of numerous bestselling books, in particular *The Sirius Mystery: New Scientific Evidence of Alien Contact 5,000 Years Ago*. Robert and I explore the scope of his work,

*April, 1968*

For as long as she could remember, Shana had been teaching herself to be content in the dark. She discovered her gift for night sight during frequent trips to the bathroom that dogged her even now that she was thirteen and no longer wet her bed. She was careful not to wake her younger sister, Missy, since their bedroom was directly beside their parents', and nobody would have a good morning if Daddy didn't get his sleep. Shana had taught herself to move mouse-like through the dark room when she needed to climb in and out of her bed, guided only by the faint blue-white glow of the moonlight through her window.

Shana's phantom vision had become so sharp over time that she could swear she saw better with her eyes *closed*, relying on other senses rather than fighting the dark. The rounded curve of her mattress, her globe-shaped bed post, the crumpled sheets—all seemed in perfect view when she touched them. That was one more odd thing about herself she could never explain to anyone, not even Missy. *No one can see with their eyes closed*, Missy would say—but Shana would almost swear on a Bible she *could*.

Even before the box arrived, Shana had begun to wonder about small ways she no longer felt quite like herself. She didn't feel quite like a regular human being—maybe she never had, as if she had accidentally found herself in a world where brown skin and white skin held such unusual importance and it was considered abnormal to see in the dark.

⊗

So, the box.

From the sight of it, the package from Aunt Priscilla might have been from the president of Mali himself. Slightly bigger than a shoebox, it arrived in the mail after school Wednesday, decorated with colorful international stickers and official red and blue stripes. *Republique du Mali*, the stamp said; it bore the image of an odd black beetle with spiny legs. Mama had set it down on the table before she called to her, as if to give her privacy with it. The package was inscribed to Shana alone—her aunt *always* included her middle name to remind her of her namesake--Miss Shana Priscilla Jackson, 500 Lauderdale Street, Memphis, Tennessee 38126.

Two smaller boxes lay inside the first box, an immediate disappointment as Shana's imagination shrank to scale. Was it jewelry? A lion's tooth? The final box, padded on all sides, was burnished metal. The latch clicked open without a key. A typed letter lay neatly folded into a thick square. When Shana lifted the letter, she found the glistening black stone beneath, an exact fit in the palm of her hand. Maybe the box had been sitting out in the sun; the stone was warm.

*Sweet Shana—I thought of you when I came across this lovely stone. I know you have loved exotic rocks since you were a baby. I was traveling with friends in the Dogon region, it's of fantastic historical importance, so you'll have to work on your French and come with me one day. The Dogon culture is quite astronomically advanced here, you know, which your American teachers will never tell you. It's a shame how they're cutting down the forests, but I found this stone near an excavation site, and I've never seen one quite like it. The geology grad students from university were very jealous of me and frantic to have it, but I hid it to send to you. If you ever tire of this, promise me you'll give it back to me when you come visit. Otherwise, keep it as my gift—and remember you come from great people who used their own science to navigate the stars.*

Aunt Priscilla always wrote as if Shana's future relied on knowing history from a continent across the ocean. And what did she mean by "navigate the stars"? Surely Aunt Priscilla didn't think Africans were exploring space like John Glenn had orbited the earth. The space flights were Shana's most fixed memories, and in some ways she felt as if she were watching the rocket's violent departure from the earth's atmosphere all the time in her mind.

Outer space was far from Memphis. Far from a country that did not love her. Unbound by gravity. Perfect.

Shana didn't often get excited about presents, but she was so happy with her mysterious new stone that she slept with it wrapped in the palm of her hand.

She was sure she saw the stone's luxuriant velvet glow even with her eyes closed.

⊗

By morning, her palm was empty. An oval-shaped shadow remained, faintly painting her palm's crevices. She patted her mattress for the stone and finally realized it was nestled in her armpit, as smooth as her own skin. To yank it free, she tugged harder than she'd thought she should have to. Removing it stung a bit, so she immediately slid it back.

"What's that?" Missy said, bounding to the foot of Shana's bed.

As Shana stared at her sister's face upturned to hers, she saw her anew: eyes starving for adventure, for relief from the constant hum about the marches and the beatings and how Larry Payne got shot. The night before, Missy had asked her, "How come they hate us so much?" and Shana couldn't find an answer. She'd told Missy to ask Mama.

Now Shana wanted to tell Missy about the stone and the stain on her palm—as a big sister, felt a *duty* to tell her. But she could not make herself say it. The words stayed coiled in her throat.

"Come on—what is it?" Missy said, insistent.

"Get off my bed!" Shana said, more angrily than she'd meant to. "Leave me alone! Why are you always bothering me?" She spoke all the words she knew Missy hated the most.

But Missy didn't storm with the anger Shana expected. Instead, tears came to Missy's eyes and her bottom lip shook. "Why are you so mean?" she said, and walked out of the room. Shana thought she heard her sob, and her throat hurt. She was near sobbing too. But not a bit of that mattered. Shana swallowed her sob and forgot it.

Image: Victor Tondee/Shutterstock.com

The stone had lost some of its coloring, so it appeared lighter than it had been when she went to sleep. *It bled*, she thought. That was when it started: her ability to understand. Shana instantly knew that she must keep the stone with her at all times and safeguard it while she slept. She must not let anyone else see it: Mama had barely given it a glance. Papa would never lay eyes on it. (How had Aunt Priscilla negotiated her way to it? Hidden it? It was remarkable.)

And she'd slept with it in her hand! She could never be that foolish again.

Her armpit was the perfect place to carry the stone—as if the crevice of warm skin were designed for the task. The long sleeves on her dress obscured the stone's bulk, and it felt so natural that Shana had to pat the spot to remember it was there. She sat with it under her arm at breakfast, where Missy sulked and wouldn't look at her. Shana was staring at her scrambled eggs thinking the word *incubation* at the moment she realized the stone's warmth matched her body temperature exactly. And the kitchen's aqua blue seemed unusually bright: the stove, the refrigerator, the sink's basin. Colors leaped at her.

Papa had a smile for them at breakfast, and smiles were rare since the strike. He'd gone to Mason Temple to hear the speech yesterday, and then he'd gone straight to bed.

"Did the Reverend give a speech, Papa?" Missy said.

Papa nodded, shoveling scrambled eggs in his mouth. He always ate in a hurry. Said he'd grown up poor with eight siblings, and if you didn't eat fast, you didn't eat.

"What'd he say?"

"Same old same old," Papa said. "Tellin' us what we already know."

"Reverend's staying at the motel, Shana, not the Holiday Inn like usual," Mama said, trying to sound casual so Papa wouldn't accuse her of worship. "So the Baileys, they want everything right to show what a Negro business can provide. Mr. Bailey asked me to put in extra hours tonight, and I want you to come help me so I'll finish by a decent hour."

Daddy was a trash collector who had never gone to college, and Aunt Priscilla thought it was scandalous that Mama was "training" Shana to be a maid; Mama being a maid was one of the things they argued about. Mama said she didn't mind cleaning when it was for Negroes, and the Baileys' motel was nicely kept up with modern décor and a colorful lighted neon sign that pointed up at the sky. The owners had named it after the song "Sweet Lorraine."

And Mama met so many people there: actors, musicians, writers. Papa complained that Mama acted like she needed to breathe the same air famous people breathed, or she didn't get enough oxygen. She was the maid supervisor and sometimes worked behind the desk, and all the famous people who stayed frequently knew her by name, so Mama was not going to leave her job at the Baileys' motel any time soon. One day Shana had passed a room and heard loud guitar licks and singing that stayed on her mind for weeks. Later, when the song "Midnight Hour" came on the radio and she knew it already, Mama only laughed and said she'd probably heard Wilson Pickett making it up through the walls. The motel was that kind of place, with music and laughing and Negroes dressed in ties and long skirts.

Still, of course Shana didn't want to go clean motel rooms after school. But she noticed the dark splotches under Mama's eyes and her gingerly movement as she walked from the counter to the table with the coffee pot to refill Papa's mug. Mama often hissed quietly when she bent over, or hummed a phrase from a freedom song to keep herself from groaning. While she'd lain curled on the ground during a sit-in in Nashville with Aunt Priscilla, a police officer had kicked them both. He'd kicked Mama's lower back, and she'd never felt right since. Having the stone helped Shana see the polished black shoe as it swung down to kick her mother with all the force the cop who wore it could muster. That was when Aunt Priscilla had left the country, and Mama had never forgiven her.

"Okay, Mama," Shana said.

"I want to go too!" Missy said. "I want to meet him."

"Just a man," Papa said. "Why make such a fuss over a regular man? He's no better'n me or you. Should have seen him sweating at the podium. He's just as scared as anyone else."

"I only need Shana, Missy," Mama said. "Bad enough for us two to be out tonight."

The curfew had been lifted Monday, but police still harassed Negroes they saw out at night. With the soldiers and the shooting, Memphis looked like

> Even before the box arrived, Shana had begun to wonder about small ways she no longer felt quite like herself. She didn't feel quite like a regular human being— maybe she never had, as if she had accidentally found herself in a world where brown skin and white skin held such unusual importance and it was considered abnormal to see in the dark.

the newscasts from Vietnam. Larry Payne, who'd been shot by police at the Reverend's march last week, was only sixteen—three years older than Shana. Papa had gone to his funeral.

"Papa, can I go too?" Missy said. "Please?"

Papa shook his head. "Just Shana." Then he turned his grave eyes up to Mama. "And don't be out late."

Shana's heart thumped with excitement as soon as she stepped outside to walk with Missy to school. Nothing was different—rows of red brick homes, neighbors climbing into their cars or walking to the bus stop, dogs barking, piles of debris on the street—but it looked new somehow. *All* of it. The stone under her arm seemed to vibrate as the expanse of the sky unfolded above her, feeding from sunlight through her skin. Blue, again: she felt like she could see through the sky. Tonight, she promised her stone, she would sleep outside.

Shana hadn't realized she'd been standing fixed on the street staring at the sky until some time had passed. She looked around, remembering herself, and saw that Missy had kept walking without her across the street to the next block. The part of her that was still Shana remembered that she had hurt her sister's feelings, and most of her still cared enough to run to catch up to her and try to say something to make amends.

She decided to talk about the things Missy was afraid of.

"I know why white folks don't treat us right," Shana said.

Despite herself, Missy was interested. The question *why* was on everyone's lips. Everyone knew how Echol Cole and Robert Walker had been crushed in the broken garbage truck, proof enough the conditions weren't fit for workers. And everyone from Thomas Jefferson to President Johnson had said all men were created equal. Everyone else knew what was right.

"They're afraid," Shana said, simplifying it best she could. "They don't want to be under us like we're under them."

"That's stupid. Ain't nobody tryin' to be over them." She and Missy said *ain't* only when Mama wasn't within hearing, thrilling with the forbidden slang. "We just don't want to be treated so mean. Like dogs. Worse than dogs."

"If it was the other way," Shana said, "we'd be the same."

"Not uh. That's stupid."

"Yes," Shana said, knowing. "We would."

"Quit trying to act like you know everything. We wouldn't never be like that. *I* wouldn't." Shana barely heard Missy, as if her sister were speaking far below her—because she could see time unlayering, unfolding—an unwrapping and redoing of things—that proved her right: that Missy's twin in that other time could be standing on the curb shouting rage as white marchers passed quietly with signs: I <u>AM</u> A MAN, which could be reduced to I <u>AM</u>. Which could be reduced to <u>I</u>. Someone very much like Missy would cheer as police officers beat them and snatched their signs away. But she would never convince Missy of what she saw.

The street's stench was stronger today. The low, sour odor that had wrapped itself around the city was unmistakable even in the morning cold. Shana's nose was separating the scents into organic, metallic and acidic, studying them with great interest, cataloguing them. (Or the stone was, anyway.) She could tell which scents were from a liquor store and which were from a butcher shop and which were from a house with a newborn or an invalid who soiled diapers or sheets beyond cleaning. If not for Missy, Shana would have stood stock still on the sidewalk with her nose turned up high to take in the smells.

Stillness felt like Shana's natural position now. To walk felt awkward, although the part of her that was Shana remembered movement fine. She more consciously monitored her movements: her steps, her breathing, her hands, her fingers. All fascinating.

And she kept noticing a number everywhere: on mailboxes, on passing buses, on car license plates: 306. The number was important somehow.

"Stinks today," Missy said. "Good. I hope nobody ever picks up the trash in this whole city. That's what they deserve."

One of the first things Shana learned about her stone was that it had a kind of unspoken language—if she squeezed her arm a certain way, or for a certain duration, she could communicate with it. This happened as Mrs. Harris called her to write on the chalk board during math—that number 306 came up again—and although Shana was right-handed, she'd foolishly chosen her right armpit to secure her stone. Wouldn't the stone fall as soon as she lifted her arm? She stammered and lied to say she didn't know how to solve the equation—but Mrs. Harris commanded her to the board. As it turned out, she shouldn't have worried: the stone burrowed so deeply in its cavern that it seemed to disappear, not moving at all when she raised her arm.

Shana perfected her language with it throughout the day: short bursts for instant clarity, a long squeeze for energy when she felt sleepy (carrying the stone *did* seem to drain her), and subtle shifts when she was curious about things that were about to happen. For instance, her sight blurred and she thought she saw Assistant Principal Gandy walk into the room to whisper in her teacher's ear—but his broad stomach did not actually appear in the doorway until seconds later.

Like Mr. Spock always said on "Star Trek," the stone was *Fascinating*.

In English, instead of copying vocabulary words from the chalkboard, Shana began documenting her new knowledge of the stone's history: *Landed three-hundred years ago as a piece of a larger mass shattered by contact with the outer atmosphere. Attracted to the Dogon region. Never touched by human hands before the forests were cut down. Remembers everything it touches.*

*Has gathered volumes of data on ants, insects, small mammals and primates. I am its first true human incubation. That powerful word again—"I."*

Shana stopped writing when her English teacher, Mrs. Hayward, rapped a ruler on her desk and snatched away her notes. Shana had a foreign impulse to take the notes back to keep the stone's secrets, but her Shana part remembered that she must not disrespect her teacher. Mrs. Hayward read the notes silently with her forehead wrinkled in a frown, but she gave the paper back. The stone helped Shana realize her teacher was actually amused—even impressed by Shana's imagination. "Write only what's on the board and stop wasting your time with silly stories," she said, and Shana said, "Yes, ma'am," as she was expected.

Then Mrs. Hayward turned to the class and asked for everyone's attention. Shana only half listened, because she had resumed writing her notes: *I will share my human data and it will teach me how to see the layers.* "Layers" wasn't the right word, exactly, but Shana was writing too quickly to be choosy. The notes were only meant to occupy her racing mind. She would not need notes. She would remember everything she learned from the stone. She would *be* the stone.

"Shana!" Mrs. Hayward scolded, and Shana laid her pen down flat. Once Shana's eyes looked up, Mrs. Hayward went on.

"Now, I've heard a rumor some of you may be planning to skip school again Friday, that there might be another march planned? If that's true, please raise your hand."

No hands went up. Shana sensed the hum of emotions around her— defiance, shyness, secretiveness, sadness. If there *were* a march, many would go. But the only plan she had overheard from Daddy was that the Reverend would lead a march on Monday.

Mrs. Hayward pursed her lips to a thin line. "Now you all listen to me," she said in a funeral director's voice, "I know everyone is excited. But you need to stay away from the marches now, hear? Some of those teenagers feel too

hopeless to think straight. And soldiers would just as soon shoot you as look at you, like this is a Tet offensive here in Memphis. We don't want anyone else getting killed. We have a national spotlight now. We don't want the world to look at Memphis and say, 'Look how they act. They cuss at police and set fires.'"

Many students nodded obediently, but they were only wearing masks like Shana, pretending she was the same Shana and nothing more. She remembered what Papa had said about the Reverend being scared. He had reason to be scared. People only set fires and cussed out police when they were scared.

Mrs. Hayward knew her students were keeping their true thoughts silent, so she only shook her head when the bell rang.

"Don't forget: we have a quiz," she said. "See you Friday."

But she would not see them Friday. Her quiz would not matter. Everyone in the class seemed to know it, but Shana knew better than anyone.

Papa had driven the Buick to work and Missy had stayed at their cousins' house after school, so Shana and Mama took the Mississippi Boulevard bus to the Patterson bus and walked the remaining blocks to the motel past decaying storefronts and boarding houses. From some distance, on Beale Street, Shana could hear raucous ghosts from years past and future. Aretha Franklin's "Chain of Fools" poured from a passing car window, and Shana nearly forgot how to walk because the music was startling: deepest grief, but also a celebration. The stone beneath her armpit burned. (Had the stone never heard music before?)

Shana patted her crease where she was carrying the stone, and it was smaller now. Shrinking. If she examined herself in her bathroom mirror later that night—if she ever looked in a mirror again—she would see a large dark spot like the one on her palm as the stone bled into her. Bled

into *them.* After today, there would be no "I."

"We're just gonna tidy the rooms where the guests checked out late and get on home," a voice said from close by. *Mama.* Shana waded out of the music's web and saw the street again, the sky's stunning light. Her mother's pearl-handled clutch purse with flower patterns swung beside her. Shana didn't dare look up at Mama's face just then because she might change her mind and fling the stone away. No one would miss her more than Mama. But Shana could never let her stone go, because it would be like letting go of a part of herself. It was too late now.

When they reached Mulberry Street, a National Guard truck rumbled by, driving slowly as if to avoid attention. The bayonets did not show like at the marches, but the truck screamed violence. A dozen soldiers watched, bored by the sight of them. They weren't much older than she was, glad to be on U.S. soil and not in a jungle. Shana noticed 306 painted at the end of a long string of numbers on the side of the truck. The stoplight blurred at the crosswalk: Shana saw the light change from red to green two-point-six seconds before her vision sharpened and the light *actually* changed.

When they reached the motel at five-thirty, the parking lot was filling up as always at the dinner hour, but most of the curtains were drawn. Shana admired the shiny white Cadillac and, beside it, an older Dodge Royal with majestic green fins. Cars fit for a king. A choir was rehearsing in one of the rooms nearby, muffled. Dazzling.

Mr. Bailey was on the phone and barely had time to speak when Mama peeked into the front office to say hello. He cupped his hand over his receiver. "Second floor," he said. "But don't bother 306." As an afterthought, he greeted Shana: "Hello, sweetheart."

"Hello, Mr. Bailey," she said, as she always did. No differently.

The cart was waiting at the top of the stairs, with its mop and broom and bucket and cleansers. Mr. Bailey didn't like the cart exposed on the balcony, where anyone could see from the parking lot and street. Quickly, Mama pushed the cart past room 306. Laughter came from inside when a man said, "I know *your* wife ain't gonna cook. She's too pretty."

They went to a room two rooms past, curtains wide open to expose the mess. Inside the room they cleaned, Shana was so distracted by the stone's explorations that Mama had to keep saying, "Hurry up," or "Go hang that up," or "Put that down," sounding more and more weary and annoyed, so Shana forced herself to forget the things the stone was studying—the temperatures and textures and scents and layers. The stale odor of cigarettes helped Shana fix herself in Now as she emptied a heap of ashes and cigarette butts into her trash bag.

She was still *Shana* enough to want to enjoy her last night with Mama, anyway.

But tonight, when her family was sleeping, she and the stone would leave the house and find a quiet place to become Shana-Stone. They would find their position to analyze and observe this world and its layers, buried somewhere in darkness, perhaps under the ground. Shana felt sadness again, but not as sharply as when she'd heard the music. She would miss her family, but not as much as she would have missed them yesterday. Or even that morning.

"Why can't grown folks remember to flush the toilet?" Mama called from the bathroom. The sound of flushing roared an echo against the wall.

"I don't know, Mama," Shana made herself say. Talking aloud was suddenly a chore.

The room was in such poor shape that cleaning it took nearly half an hour. Mama fretted over how late they would get home as she rolled the cart back outside, where the daylight was waning in a furious orange fireball to the west. A ruckus raged in the parking lot below, the sound of milling and preparation. A few voices still sang, practicing spirituals in harmony.

Behind them, a man on the balcony was laughing. The stone was especially intrigued by laughter, so Shana turned

and saw that the door to 306 yawned wide open. She knew the face of the man standing outside of the room near the railing. He was wearing a suit and tie, as if he were already dressed for a funeral.

It was the Reverend. His face was familiar from the news even if she'd had no stone to tell her. The burning in her armpit flared, and Shana allowed herself to see the layers that were always present, the different versions of Now: she and her stone were witnesses, as her stone had witnessed for hundreds of years before she'd been born.

"Doc!" a voice called from downstairs. "You remember Ben? Ben Branch?"

The Reverend grinned and waved to the parking lot below. "Hey—how are you?" Excitement lighted his face as he leaned over the railing. "Tonight, be sure you play 'Precious Lord, Take My Hand.' Do it real pretty, now."

Downstairs, more laughter. "I will, Doc. I will."

As Shana and her stone—the Shana-Stone—studied the layers, the balcony blurred. Shana-Stone heard the gunshot three-point-two seconds before the gunman down the street squeezed the trigger. They heard before Mrs. Bailey would hear it and fall, shocked to the point of having a stroke. They heard before anyone would duck for cover or point out where the fearsome sound had been born. The layers unfolded in a blizzard.

"It's cold tonight!" another man called up. "Don't ya'll forget your coats."

The gunshot had not yet come. Mrs. Bailey was on her feet and the city wasn't burning and the Reverend was still smiling. Downstairs, a girl who sounded Missy's age giggled wildly.

The part of Shana that was still Shana called out: "Reverend!"

Her voice was loud. Mama's hand tightened on Shana's shoulder, warning her to hush and not be a bother. The Reverend's head moved one-and-three-quarters of an inch to the right when he turned to her. His widening smile at her was cut short by the gunshot.

As they remembered everything,

Shana-Stone would never forget the look of resignation on the Reverend's face when the window to room 306 shattered behind him, or how his shoulders hunched high as he waited for a second shot to come. Or the way he crouched back against the wall like a child, his arms wrapped over his head amidst the shouting and screaming. Or his panting voice as men scrambled from the room to see after him: "I'm okay. I'm okay."

Shana-Stone could see the layers: others would try to kill him. Violence was the humans' tradition, and the end of one Now led to another. The Reverend had confessed to Daddy and everyone else gathered at Mason Temple last night that he knew his time had come. Daddy never told them at the breakfast table, but he'd cried himself to sleep after the speech.

For the briefest instant, Shana-Stone wondered if calling out to the Reverend had been a mistake—because *their* way, Shana-Stone, was stillness. They were witnesses.

But until her final shift, a piece of Shana-Stone was only Shana. Human. And humans were never still—they were always in motion—even in their sleep.

That was one of the first things the stone had learned about Shana. ●

"It was a huge thing, reaching almost to the ceiling. But it was of a curious composition: it was made of skin and naked flesh, and on top there was something like a rounded head with no face and no hair. On the very top of the head was a single eye, gazing motionlessly upward."
— Carl Jung's phallic vision

Phallic pillar, Ireland

# CARL JUNG

# AND THE LIGHTS IN THE SKY

BY DONALD TYSON

### Foo Fighters

When seeking to understand any subject that has grown over the years into a complex and bewildering branching of topics and subtopics, it is sometimes useful to go back to its simple beginning, and examine its seminal root.

It's generally agreed that the UFO phenomenon began toward the end of the Second World War, when Allied pilots flying over Europe reported seeing strange lights in the sky. The lights, which were usually red, yellow or orange in color, came to be known as "foo fighters." They would sometimes follow the Allied planes, race past them, fly around them, and appeared in some way to be interested

in or attracted to them.

When the war came to an end, for a short time sightings of these strange lights seemed to recede, but then in the summer of 1947 they began to be reported in the skies over America. Civilian aviator Kenneth Arnold reported seeing nine disk-shaped objects flying in formation over Mount Rainier in Washington. Soon people all around the world were seeing them. In 1953 the United States Air Force gave them the official designation of "unidentified flying objects" or UFOs.

### Vision of a Phallic Pillar

The sightings attracted the interest of Carl Jung (1875-1961), the father of Jungian psychology, who was then widely

regarded as one of the greatest living intellectuals. By the time of the UFO craze Jung was an old man, although his intellectual faculties were undiminished. In 1947 he began to collect books on the subject. The sheer strangeness of the moving lights in the sky appealed to him. Throughout his life he had been fascinated by the fanciful, the bizarre, the unexplained.

Born during the heart of the Victorian Age, when he was a boy of three or four Jung experienced a strange dream that became the driving force that shaped his entire life, and caused him to devote himself to a study of visions, dreams, symbolism, and mythology.

He dreamed that he descended under the earth to a chamber with a flagstone

**Cigar-shaped UFO**

floor and an arched stone roof. From the archway through which he entered, a red carpet ran across the chamber to a golden throne. Upon the seat of the throne stood a round pillar that seemed to be twelve to fifteen feet tall. I'll let Jung describe it in his own words:

> *It was a huge thing, reaching almost to the ceiling. But it was of a curious composition: it was made of skin and naked flesh, and on top there was something like a rounded head with no face and no hair. On the very top of the head was a single eye, gazing motionlessly upward.*
> (Jung. *Memories, Dreams, Reflections.* New York: Vintage Books, 1963, p. 12.)

The vision terrified him. For many nights he was afraid to go to sleep for fear he would have the dream again. It was only years later that he realized that the enthroned pillar was a "ritual phallus." He became obsessed with understanding the meaning of the dream. Thus began his career as an analyst of dreams, visions, and symbols.

In 1907 Jung met Sigmund Freud and began to collaborate with him and to use Freud's new system of psychotherapy, but eventually he was forced to stop using Freud's methods because he found them inadequate to describe the mysteries of the human mind. Freud, Jung came to believe, placed too much emphasis on the importance of sexuality. Jung preferred to focus his attention on the images that arose from what Jung called the collective unconscious—a repository of primal symbols shared by the entire human race. He developed his own system of psychoanalysis that relied on an analysis of dream imagery and symbolism.

In spite of his immense popularity, Jung was always highly controversial, for one simple reason—he was not a materialist. He accepted the reality of psychic abilities, and he recognized that the spiritual aspect of human nature was at least as important as the physical part. He believed in something he called race memory, which was stored in the collective unconscious, and also in the meaningfulness of significantly connected but causally unrelated events, for which he coined the term "synchronicities." Another name for induced synchronicities is magic. Five hundred years ago Jung would have been burned at the stake as a necromancer.

***Jung's Fascination with UFOs***

Other academics and scientists shied away from the subject of UFOs. There was too great a chance of being mocked, of losing their professional credibility, merely by showing an interest in the subject. But not Jung. He had spent decades studying the intricate and complex symbolism of alchemy, a subject no scientist of his day would dare to touch other than to reject it as a folly of less enlightened times, so the likelihood of being mocked did not deter him. He had already been scoffed at and rejected by the majority of physical scientists because his ideas about archetypes, the animus and anima, synchronicity, and the racial unconscious could not be proven to have validity by scientific methods.

Jung's fascination with the UFO phenomenon was heightened by his suspicion that the lights in the sky were a warning to humanity of some unseen but dire catastrophe that was coming in the near future. He suspected that they might be a kind of alarm bell being sounded throughout humanity by the collective unconscious.

As the decade of the 1950s dawned, there were two factors affecting the fate of humanity that deeply concerned Jung. One was the tension provoked by what Winston Churchill had called "the Iron Curtain"—the political divide between America and the Soviet Union. The Soviets had set off their first atomic bomb in 1949. The threat of a war of nuclear annihilation was looming ever larger in the minds of Westerners.

The other fateful factor of concern was more esoteric but no less real to Jung—the turning of what Jung called the "Platonic month," an astrological age defined by the span of the signs of the zodiac. It takes approximately 2160 years for the point of the spring equinox to work its way through each zodiac sign. The sign defines the age in which we presently live. For the past two millennia we have been living in the Age of Pisces, but we are presently transitioning into the next age, the Age of

Aquarius. The exact year of that transition is not known but it is generally agreed that we are still moving into the next astrological age.

Jung was well aware of the risk to his professional reputation that he was taking by drawing attention to the importance of this cosmic transition. However, he felt that the UFO phenomenon was too ominous to ignore. He wrote:

*It would be frivolous of me to try to conceal from the reader that such reflections are not only exceedingly unpopular but come perilously close to those turbid fantasies which becloud the minds of world-reformers and other interpreters of "signs and portents." But I must take this risk, even if it means putting my hard-won reputation for truthfulness, reliability, and capacity for scientific judgment in jeopardy. I can assure my readers that I do not*

*do this with a light heart. I am, to be quite frank, concerned for all those who are caught unprepared by the events in question and disconcerted by their incomprehensible nature. Since, so far as I know, no one has yet felt moved to examine and set forth the possible psychic consequences of this foreseeable astrological change, I deem it my duty to do what I can in this respect.*
(Jung. *Flying Saucers.* New York: MJF Books, 1978, p. 6.)

This deep concern for the welfare of the human race caused him to write a book about UFOs. Throughout the decade of the fifties he studied UFOs and gathered source information on them, and in 1958 he published his book in the German language. The following year it was translated into English by R. F. C. Hull under the title *Flying Saucers: A Modern Myth of Things Seen in the Skies.*

## Eye of God seen in the sky

**Nuremberg broadsheet, 1561, showing globes, tubes and other objects in the sky**

### The Real and the Unreal

Today, the subject of UFOs has evolved into a bewildering array of connected topics, among them close encounters, alien abductions, alien races, alien technology, implants, alien rape, human-alien hybrids, men in black, reptilians, greys, and black oil, to list by no means all of them. But we are interested in the roots of UFOs, so we must remind ourselves that when Carl Jung began to apply his extraordinary intellect in an effort to determine their significance, UFOs were exactly that—

unidentified flying objects.

In his preface to the English edition of his book, Jung made the point that he was not one of the true believers who felt that flying saucers, as they were sometimes called, were real physical objects. Because he wrote about the subject sympathetically, UFO fanatics were quick to embrace him as one of their own. He noted that it was a lot easier to be a believer than a sceptic.

*To believe that UFOs are real suits the general opinion, whereas disbelief is to be discouraged. This creates the impression that there is a tendency all over the world to believe in saucers and to want them to be real, unconsciously helped along by a press that otherwise has no sympathy with the phenomenon.*
(Jung, *Flying Saucers*, p. 3)

Jung called the saucer craze a "living myth" and observed, "We have here a golden opportunity to see how a legend is formed, and how in a difficult and dark time for humanity a miraculous tale grows up of an attempted intervention by extraterrestrial 'heavenly' powers—and this at the very time when human fantasy is seriously considering the possibility of space travel and of visiting or even invading other planets." (Jung, *Flying Saucers*, pp. 16-7)

Let me set forth Jung's beliefs about the reality of UFOs here so there will be no misunderstanding of the kind that was so common during his lifetime. He was perfectly convinced that UFOs were real, but was not convinced that they were physical. To Jung, a thing did not need to be material to be real. He considered the archetypes in the unconscious to be just as real as rocks and trees, even though they have no material substance. In his book he wrote:

*For in the common estimation a subjective observation can only be either "true" or else, as a delusion of the senses or an hallucination, it can only be "untrue." The fact that the latter are also true phenomena with sufficient reasons of their own is apparently never taken into account, so long as no obvious pathological disturbance is present. There are, however, manifestations of the unconscious, even in normal people, which can be so "real" and impressive that the observer instinctively resists taking his perception as a delusion or hallucination.* (Jung, *Flying Saucers*, p. 71)

At the same time, Jung felt he could not avoid accepting that something that gave rise to UFOs was both real and physical, due to the many eyewitness accounts of lights in the sky and their simultaneous tracking by radar instillations. But he did not necessarily believe that what was picked up by radar were the UFOs themselves. He thought that synchronicity might be involved, and alluded to the possible role of the kind of ESP abilities then being studied by J. B. Rhine at Duke University. Jung did believe without equivocation in ESP, which he referred to as "meaningful

coincidences, i.e., acausal, synchronistic phenomena." (Jung, *Flying Saucers*, p. 43)

He summed up his position by saying that it was the same as that of Edward J. Ruppelt, former chief of the USAF's project for investigating UFO reports. Referring to Ruppelt's 1956 *Report on Unidentified Flying Objects*, Jung gave both their conclusions as "*something is seen, but one doesn't know what.*" (Jung, *Flying Saucers*, p. 6)

UFOs may be purely physical, they may be psychological, or they may be psychological but evoked by something physical. When wrestling with the radar evidence, Jung was moved to remark, "It boils down to nothing less than this: that either psychic projections throw

**Carl Jung (1875-1961) - Psychologist, Psychiatrist, Author, Artist, Visionary**

back a radar echo, or else the appearance of real objects affords an opportunity for mythological projections." (*Flying Saucers*, p. 107)

### Unidentified Flying Objects

Jung's psychological analysis of the nature of UFOs is based on the earliest sightings, when these flying saucers were no more than things seen in the sky. The very fact that they are in the sky is significant, because the heavens

are the place of God. This suggests that they are divine portents. Jung also found great significance in their shapes, which were usually round. Roundness signifies completeness, and is the shape of the archetypal symbols known as mandalas, another indication that the UFOs have a higher significance. Mandalas signify the totality of the self, both its unconscious and its conscious sides. The circle is a symbol of order, and of the soul. Jung also connected this round shape with the "eye of God." (Jung, *Flying Saucers*, pp. 31, 80)

A less common shape observed in the early years of UFO sightings was like a cigar—cylindrical and rounded on the ends. The cigar-shaped UFOs were said to hold many smaller disk-shaped UFOs within them, which would fly out, and for this reason where called the "mother ships." Anyone who has seen the David Lynch movie version of *Dune* will recognize these two seminal shapes in the scene where the great, cigar-shaped mother ship folds space with the many smaller disk-shaped or lens-shaped craft nestled safely inside it.

In passing Jung mentions that one may draw a sexual connection with these two shapes, the cigar shape corresponding with the male penis, and the lens shape (created when the circular UFO is seen from the side) with the vagina. However, this is more Freudian than Jungian, and Jung does not make much out of it.

He is more interested in how the UFOs fly through the air. Various accounts describe them as darting one way and another, stopping to hover motionless in the air, and then flying off at incredible speed. Jung rightly observed that if any physical craft made such sharp manoeuvres, or accelerated and decelerated at such a rate, the G-forces involved would certainly kill any living thing inside it. He called the motions of UFOs "weightless." He speculated about anti-gravity—if the flying disks are ships from another planet, perhaps their crews have discovered how to manipulate gravity.

**Basel woodcut, 1566, showing black globes in the sky**

More than anything else, the way in which the lights or saucers flew through the sky struck Jung as insect-like. They darted here and there, and hovered, just as insects do. Sometimes they surrounded a place and appear to be interested in it, before darting off again. For this reason they could not be meteors or reflections from temperature inversion layers.

In the later years of his investigation of UFOs Jung became aware of the various types of aliens who have been seen by those who claim to have had close encounters.

*These space-guests are sometimes idealized figures along the lines of technological angels who are concerned for our welfare, sometimes dwarfs with enormous heads bursting with intelligence, sometimes lemur-like creatures covered with hair, and equipped with claws, or dwarfish monsters clad in armour and looking like insects.*
(Jung, *Flying Saucers*, p. 16)

He also mentioned that the inhabitants of the saucers were sometimes of human shape, but only three feet tall, or on other occasions fifteen feet tall.

### Analysis of UFOs

Jung proceeded to analyse UFOs in the way in which he was most familiar— by examining UFO-like imagery that appeared in his patients' dreams. These symbols appeared in the dreams even of those with no interest in the UFO craze, and were not recognized by the dreamers themselves as UFOs. Jung gave a detailed analysis of seven dreams, along with the commentaries on them by the dreamers.

He also gave consideration to the sightings of lights and other portents in the sky that have occurred throughout human history, long before they were called UFOs. There have always been sightings of wonders in the heavens, usually at times of great importance or tension. He quotes Samuel Coccius, a 16th century arts student at Basel, in Switzerland, that on August 7, 1566,

"many large black globes were seen in the air, moving before the sun with great speed, and turning against each other as if fighting. Some of them became red and fiery and afterwards faded and went out." (Jung, *Flying Saucers*, p. 95) This sighting was illustrated by a woodcut.

Concerning this vision in the sky, it might be pointed out that by staring up at the sun, black spots would be temporarily impressed on the retina of the eye, causing the observer to see multiple black circles that would appear to move about when the eye was moved. However, this is my observation, not Jung's. He was not so much concerned with the source that generated the vision as he was with the symbolic content of the vision.

Jung mentioned another mass sighting that was illustrated by a woodcut, this one having taken place at Nuremberg in 1561. Numerous men and women of the town looked up at sunrise on April 14 of that year, and saw large numbers of blood-red, bluish or black globes near the sun. They also saw two great tubes "in which three,

Saucer-shaped UFO

four and more globes were to be seen."
(Jung, *Flying Saucers*, p. 96) Underneath
these globes and tubes there was a long
object "shaped like a great black spear."
After about an hour all these things fell
to the earth and slowly faded away.

Again, it seems to me that such
artefacts of vision might well be generated
by staring too long at the sun. I find it
significant that the sun is specifically
mentioned in the accounts of both the
mass vision of 1561 and that of 1566.
But Jung was more concerned with the
meaning of the visions, not their origins.
He observed that the tubes described
with disks inside them were like the
UFO mother ships. Concerning the
globes, he wrote, "If the UFOs were living
organisms, one would think of a swarm
of insects rising with the sun, not to fight
one another but to mate and celebrate the
marriage flight." (Jung, *Flying Saucers*, p.
96)

### A Warning to Mankind

Although Jung was obviously
fascinated by UFO sightings for the
way their symbols revealed the workings
of the unconscious mind, that was not
what caused him to write his highly
controversial book, which he feared
might even be career destroying. He felt
compelled to write the book as a warning

to mankind. The nuclear stalemate
between the United States and what was
then the USSR had created a perilous
situation of an order of magnitude never
before seen in human history. We were
(and still are, for that matter) actually
facing a possible extinction-level event.

Jung wrote, "The present world
situation is calculated as never before
to arouse expectations of a redeeming,
supernatural event." (Jung, *Flying Saucers*,
p. 22) However, our modern materialistic
viewpoint in the West has caused us
to dismiss anything that is considered
unscientific. Science has replaced
Christianity as the repository of our faith
in the future.

*Desperate efforts are made for a
"repristination" of our Christian
faith, but we cannot get back to that
limited world view which in former
times left room for metaphysical
intervention. Nor can we resuscitate
a genuine Christian believe in an
after-life or the equally Christian
hope for an imminent end of the
world that would put a definite stop
to the regrettable error of Creation.
Belief in this world and in the power
of man has, despite assurances to the
contrary, become a practical and, for
the time being, irrefragable truth.
(Jung, Flying Saucers, p. 22)*

This loss of religious faith has caused
the great upwelling of the collective
unconsciousness represented by the UFO
phenomenon to assume a more scientific,
physical character than it would have
assumed in earlier centuries. "Anything
that looks technological goes down
without difficulty with modern man.
The possibility of space travel has made
the unpopular idea of a metaphysical
intervention much more acceptable."
(Jung, *Flying Saucers*, pp. 22-3)

It was the sheer magnitude of the UFO
phenomenon that most alarmed Jung.
He saw it as the voice of the collective
unconscious of the human race crying out
a warning of some imminent catastrophe
that could only be remedied by a radical
shift in human consciousness. Jung did
not specify the nature of the disaster, but
did refer to the Cold War in an oblique
way. He may have had in mind something
not unlike the Cuban Missile Crisis of
October 16-28, 1962, which he did not
live to experience, in which America and
the USSR stood on the very brink of
mutual nuclear destruction. Fortunately
for us all, our annihilation was averted on
that occasion, but whether this was due to
a divine intervention or merely a moment
of scientific rationality on the part of the
leaders of both empires is moot. ◗

# ATEUCHUS

## BY PHILIP FRACASSI

*"I am a worm and not a man..."*
Psalm 22:6 (attributed to Jesus)

**1**

Alfie drove the Jeep hard over the rough, rock-strewn road that led to the find. He was up high now, altitude of at least 10,000 feet, the wind brittle cold. He kept the windows down, enjoying it, relishing the clean air, even if it turned his knuckles to blue bolts as they held the steering wheel.

The Jeep lifted high on the passenger side, came down with a thud, then dipped left into a gulley, rocking Alfie so hard his feet momentarily left the pedals. He jerked back into the seat, laughed, and gave it more gas.

James had said "not of this earth," and James—an Oxford man through and through—wasn't one for hyperbole or metaphor. Quite literal, his geologist friend. He'd also said the sample showed dramatic aging that held no relation to its geological position or depth. Put the two together and you had a nice fat meteorite, a juicy bit of space right here on planet Utah, only a few hours' drive for Alfie from his home-based lab near the university. He praised the heavens the thing wasn't found a bit further north, across the border, or James might have been calling Jim Robinson at Wyoming instead. Even so, Alfie figured the find was technically on federal land, part of Ashley National Park, but he wasn't about to bring that up with James. Hell no, this space rock was his and by God he meant to have it.

The Jeep bounced over a ridge and Alfie saw the tents in the distance, navy green pimples dotted along a butte a half-mile ahead, the thin dirt road twisting like a brown snake right for it.

"About five-thousand years, I'd say,

More or less. Just a baby, really."

Alfie nodded, stared at the blackened chunk of rock lying in the middle of the miniature crater the geologists had dug around it. Its surface was jagged, almost crystallized, and gave off a black, chalky residue when touched. It looked, to Alfie anyway, rather unstable. More like shale than stone. James's crew, all students, stood absently around the dig, some of them likely hoping to be included in whatever this discovery ended up being, the rest simply cold and homesick. Alfie smirked, remembering his own years as a student, having to take whatever shit the professor or project head doled out.

*Hate to break it to you, fellas, but your claim on this meteorite went out the window when your boss brought my sorry ass up this mountain*, he thought, itching to be gone but not wanting to seem overly anxious, lest James rethink the importance of the discovery.

"Pre-Egyptian," Alfie mused, as if bored, each word punctuated by clouds of breath in the frigid air. "Any similarities?"

James jammed his thin white hands into the front pockets of his vest to warm them, stuck out his lower lip. A posture he took often, and one that Alfie always thought would go well with a pipe and a stuffed hawk in the

background, decorating the mahogany of whatever Oxford study room James most often postured within.

"Nothing on record, not anything like this, at least. She's a rare bird. The composition is strange for a meteorite. As you can see it's flaking, oxidization must have been slowly cooking this thing for the last few millennia, killing it from the inside out. But like I said, the material is completely alien. I may not know much about this little guy, but I know it wasn't born on planet earth. I've already taken my samples, pictures, measured, weighed, catalogued. It's not a chondrite, I can tell you… some rare achondrite I've never come across, and since you're the only meteoritic within a thousand miles, I figured I'd hand you the baton. I have my hands full with the shit I actually came out here to do."

Alfie nodded, only half-listening, not entirely caring about James's considerations on the matter, since the man knew as much about meteorology as Alfie knew, or cared, about the archeologic bone-digging mission the Brits were on about. Besides, he was entranced by the object before him; it consumed every ounce of his attention. "Iron prominent, I assume?" he asked, knowing the answer but wanting to build some goodwill by asking the idiot his opinion.

James looked at him strangely, his voice lowering, as if nervous of being overheard. "That's the thing, Alfie. You'd think it'd be packed with ferrous, yeah? But it's not. So far, our tests have shown no iron at all."

Alfie gave him a hard look. "You've got to be mistaken."

James scoffed, pulled the front of his khaki archeologist vest down neatly. "I don't think so. If there's one thing I know, it's how to test the chemical makeup of rock. Or, in this case, meteorite. Ergo, I'm curious what the university will come up with."

Alfie nodded. "Well, I better load up and get it over there. People are waiting to see this baby," he said, knowing damn well he had no plans to take the find anywhere but his own home lab. He didn't want—or need—the university's premature meddling in a case like this one. If he was ever going to raise his personal profile within the scientific community, he knew it had to be outside the purview of his employer. He stepped down into the belly of the crater the team had dug out, his eyes dancing over the rock in anticipation.

*You ready to go home?* he thought, kneeling down beside the meteorite, about the size and shape of two bowling balls side-by-side, joined at the corpulent hip. He rubbed the surface with his fingertips, gave a little yelp and flinched, jerked his hand away. He could have sworn he felt a *pulse*, like he had touched an electrical wire thrumming with current—not enough

to shock, but enough to make him want his fingers back, thanks very much.

He stared at the black smudges on his fingertips, rubbed them together, the dust staining his skin. His hands were trembling.

"Don't tell me it shocked you, mate. I'll have to call the Star," James said without humor.

"No, it's fine," Alfie said, the strangeness of the meteorite only building his excitement to study it more closely. "You're the composition expert, so tell me. What's it made of?"

"Beats me," James said irritably, beckoning for two nearby assistants to come over and help with load-in. "What the hell you think I called you for?"

### 2

Alfie dollied the large, latched titanium case through the front double-doors of his slate-gray home, the 201 freeway roaring above and behind him as he weaved the hand truck through the entry and into the carpeted living room, rumbled over the linoleum kitchen floor and slowly lowered the hand truck's wheels down the basement stairs to his lab, step-by-step, careful not to jostle the crate's docile contents despite knowing the case's interior padding held the meteorite firmly in place.

He set the case in the middle of the lab floor, turned on all the lights and ran back up the stairs, nearly bursting with anticipation. He was sure *this* would be the Big One that finally raised his profile to national, if not global, heights. He imagined the grants pouring in, the book offers and, inevitably, the substantial raise in salary from the university. That's if they could even keep him, of course! He had, after all, always enjoyed the idea of an Ivy League professorship, and there was always MIT. Why *not* dream big?

Outside, Alfie closed and locked up the Jeep, then ran back inside, where he hurriedly closed and locked the front doors. As he flipped the deadbolt he gave one last look outside through the door's small window. His front yard,

a large half-acre weed-riddled thing surrounded by a low metal fence, and the giant, adjacent vacant dirt lot that served as his only neighbor, were both as empty and quiet as ever. Chastising himself for his paranoia, he turned and strode deliberately for the stairs.

Midway there he changed his mind and went through the living room to the glass double-doors leading to the rear of the house. He checked the backyard, found it clear, then locked the sliding doors, pulled the brown woolen curtains closed, robbing the room of light, leaving him in musty darkness.

He diligently went through the rest of the house, pulled every curtain, closed every blind. On his way to the basement, he activated the door alarm, the one he usually only set when travelling.

Just in case.

⊗

Alfie had converted the basement a few years back, having realized he could get more work done—without prying eyes constantly peering greedily over his shoulder—in the privacy of his own home. He'd installed a reinforced metal door with a deadbolt lock, put up fluorescent lights throughout, dry-walled over the exposed beams and painted it all a stark, lab-white. He'd built in an industrial washing station at one end of the open room, an end-to-end stainless steel countertop along the adjacent wall, mounted cabinetry above, and purchased two mortician tables that he'd wheeled together to form a workstation in the center.

It was upon the mortician tables (thoroughly steel-brushed and sanitized once purchased) that he placed the meteorite for inspection.

Alfie checked the two digital cameras mounted to the walls— one above the counter, one on the opposite wall—and made sure they were recording to a massive terabyte cloud drive the university provided. Satisfied everything was in order, he donned goggles and surgical gloves, then approached the meteorite. He shifted the rock a bit so it rested easily on the table, without any wobble, and prepared for testing.

Using his lightest rock hammer, he chipped a fragment off the side of the dusty black rock, then another, and another. Enough to get started. He put the respective samples in their own enclosed petri dishes, labeled them One, Two and Three. He walked them to the counter where his equipment was set up, including a microscope (on loan from the university), a series of acids and solvents, brushes and fine tools and other refined equipment, some of which was his, most of which he had borrowed and not yet returned.

"One more, I think," he said, wanting to test a particular oxygen generator mixture on a clean sample. He turned, hammer in hand, back toward the meteorite. And froze.

A thick, wriggling, maggot-like creature, white as a sunken corpse, slick with moisture and peppered with dusty black residue, protruded from a crack in the rock, the exact spot where he had chipped away his last sample.

At first, he assumed the thing must have been somehow attached to the *exterior* of the rock, something he had missed while packing and pulling it from the crate. *Something James missed while taking his measurements and weights and pictures? Fat chance.*

He stepped closer to the meteorite, spun the table slightly on its smooth wheels in order to get a better view of the entire surface without having to touch it. He fully expected to see the worm sticking to the side of the meteorite.

But it wasn't.

It was obviously—quite unbelievably—pushing its way outward from *inside* the rock.

"Impossible," he muttered, his mind already racing for explanations, scientific rationale for how the worm might have been trapped inside the meteorite... possibly trapped under years of sedimentation, perhaps as other materials had slowly built themselves up around the surface, somehow trapping... *alive*... this creature... or its initial heat melting surrounding matter to its core... or something may have

burrowed itself *into* the rock... laid eggs...

Alfie knew how ridiculous this all was.

But not, however, as ridiculous as the alternative. That the worm had been living inside the rock for, what, five-thousand years? That it had been inside while the thing hurled through space for who knew how long? Impossible! Ludicrous! Nothing could survive, especially something that appeared to be in its larva state... just recently hatched...

*Unless.*

Unless there were eggs inside the meteorite that were dormant. Somehow... suspended. And then, perhaps... just perhaps... when supplied with a certain life-giving element... namely oxygen... a *trigger.*

Alfie bent over, his face less than a foot from where the larva slowly, persistently, pushed itself through a small, almost invisible, crack in the shell. A syrupy clear residue leaked down the black surface of the rock as the larva continued to thrust its way into the world. *Into our world,* Alfie thought... and the ramifications of this discovery suddenly exploded in his mind.

His back straightened. Behind the goggles, his eyes grew wide. His body went a tingly sort of numb all over. He realized, with stunned wonderment, exactly what may have just happened inside the basement of his home.

*His* home. In *his* laboratory.

*Alien life,* he thought dumbly, drunkenly.

"I've discovered alien life," he said aloud, testing the words, the idea. *Maybe I have...* He looked at the worm once more. Nothing else made sense. He knew it in his heart, in his scientific mind... there was no other possibility.

Like a stretched piece of elastic, his mind snapped into place, his body rediscovered its nerve endings, and the whole world glowed with brilliant possibilities. "HOLY SHIT!" he screamed, and spun in a circle, dropped the hammer to the floor, ripped off his goggles and howled at the ceiling, "WOO-HOO!! Alien life, baby!"

He laughed loudly, hysterically, then caught himself, realized he was drooling, breathing heavy, his heart pounding. He wiped his mouth, stared at the worm still extracting itself, his face hurting from grinning too hard. He rubbed at his stubbly cheeks.

"Get a grip, Alfie," he said, realizing there was a mile of testing and analysis before even considering such a wild claim. He would have to be sure. Unequivocally, undeniably, *positively* sure. If he revealed his finding and was wrong he would be the laughing stock of the scientific community. He would be done, finished. So yes, he must be *absolutely* sure...

*Oh, yeah...* he thought, *but what IF!*

"I'll be famous," he said, addressing the visitor, who didn't seem to care or notice Alfie's state of pure exaltation. "I'd be the most famous person in the world," he said, slowly and surely, tasting each syllable as it rolled off his tongue.

"Okay, okay," he said, trying to calm himself, to slow the rush of blood to his head, the adrenaline-fueled pumping of his heart, and focus as best he could. "First things first," he said, and took a deep breath. "My little friend, I'm gonna need you to put on your game face."

Alfie ran a hand through his hair, cleared his throat, and stepped up to one of the mounted cameras. Assured by the red light, he looked directly into the lens and began to speak.

"My name is Alfred James Monroe. It is August 21st, 2016. I have recently returned from a sample-gathering trip near Athena National Forest, just *outside* the federal perimeter, where I discovered what I immediately deduced to be a meteorite. Subsequently, I brought the meteorite back to my lab for further study and, in order to analyze samples of the rock, I proceeded to chip off a sample of the exterior shell. Having done this, in no great extreme, I produced what appeared to be a small fissure leading to a hollow in the interior of the meteorite. Stunning, I realize." He paused for effect. "Even more stunning, and still hard to believe, is what's inside."

He turned slowly, hand laid out like a game show model revealing the Grand Prize, letting the tension build for future generations, and pointed at the white, fat larva. As the camera recorded the moment for posterity, the larva finished its expulsive journey through the rock's shell and fell with an inglorious *plop* to the lab table's surface, a trail of clear goo thin as a spider web thread stretched between it and the hole it had burrowed through.

"Shit!" Alfie yelled, immediately forgetting the camera and lunging for one of the petri dishes and a glass stirring rod on the counter behind him. Grabbing the items, he spun back to the steel table on which the meteorite sat and gently—*oh so gently*—rolled the larva into the petri dish where it lay, relatively docile, slowly squirming and bending this way and that.

"Hello," Alfie said, mesmerized, holding the clear dish and its lone occupant so close to his face he could almost smell its dank alien excretion. "My name's Alfie, what's yours?" he said, and laughed at his own stupidity. "I'm sorry? What was that?" he said, putting the thing in the dish close to his ear, "it's hard to hear you because you're so very small. Wait, let me guess," he said, setting the dish down on the work table, anxious to get a closer look, "take me to your leader, am I right?"

The larva squirmed like a living slick white thumb as Alfie put it under the microscope, beyond curious to know the detailed makeup of the alien creature. He would need to extract tissue, study its composition. He'd have to send it off for analysis, but how to do it without letting the proverbial cat out of the bag? He shook his head. *A problem for another time.* Then he stuck his eye to the microscope's eyepiece, his hand absently reaching for a notepad and pencil.

"Rub-a-dub-dub, there's a grub in my tub..." he mumbled, making notes.

He was so immersed in studying the alien creature that Alfie did not see the emergence of a second larva head protruding from the same slick crack of the meteorite, pushing its way stubbornly, and with great purpose, toward the new world.

### 3

In the days that followed, Alfie was forced to leave the house twice for supplies and equipment. Otherwise, he did not sleep, or shower, and hardly ate. He had called his supervising professor at the university and given a cock-and-bull story about his mother (long deceased) being gravely ill, saying that he'd be leaving town a few days, maybe a week, maybe longer. The professor had given his regards and assured Alfie to take all the time necessary. Which was just peachy for Alfie, because since that first larva had poked its head out from the meteorite, he had forgotten about anything other than studying the strange creatures, going through the identification process, and seeking madly to positively identify them as truly, undeniably, extraterrestrial in origin.

Now, as he stood and stretched after a short nap on the cold steel mortician's table adjacent to the one that held the meteorite, Alfie thought the lab looked more and more like an incubation chamber. There were six rectangular aquariums lined along the full-length of the counter, each holding about a dozen of the alien larvae. He had filled each aquarium halfway with thick, dense black soil, roots and other vegetation, hoping the creatures would be able to feed off the earthen offerings.

After those first two larvae had wriggled free of the meteorite, many more followed, and followed, and followed. He decided to cut to the chase and, as delicately as he could, split the rock with a hammer and chisel. Inside he had found two nests, each containing a giant's fist of squiggling, slimy larvae, feeding themselves on the carcasses of who Alfie assumed had been their parents, for lack of a better label. Once he had moved each of the larvae to the incubation aquariums, he was able to better study the remaining husks of the host creatures.

His initial thought, followed quickly by a stomach-dipping surge of disappointment, was that they weren't alien creatures at all.

They were beetles.

Large beetles to be sure, and most closely resembling the *scarabaeidae* or, more commonly known, Scarab beetle. The carapaces were a foot in length, wide as a hand, and heavy as brick. Alfie was no entomologist, but he knew enough about the science of insects to know the hosts had likely given birth only very recently, possibly upon the discovery by James and his team just a week or so prior. *Something triggered the birthing process,* he thought again, knowing it impossible but too intrigued to let it go. *Like they were waiting, dormant, in some sort of hibernation...*

Alfie allowed the scenario to work its way around his head as he studied the creatures, whose biology was so similar, but also so very different—very *alien*—from earth's own insects.

They were much denser, for one. The gravity on the world they came from must be vastly different from Earth's, and when he looked at the meteorite he began to think of it less as a rock and more of a spaceship of sorts, despite it being composed of mineral versus machine. Primitive, and yet, somehow, superior to man's technology. It had landed five thousand years ago, struck the earth hard enough to be deeply buried, hidden, all that time. What remained of it, anyway; what hadn't burnt to ash upon entry through earth's atmosphere. And there the inhabitants had lain, for thousands of years, awaiting discovery...

*Awaiting release.*

He knew it was true. There are no coincidences in science. The beings had lain stagnant, been unearthed, and when something released inside the chambers... a ticking clock had begun. The four creatures, a male and female, for lack of a better understanding, two in each chamber, had procreated, laid eggs... given birth to the masses of larvae, then been slowly consumed by them, nourishing the offspring with their own flesh until the time for release came.

A release Alfie had single-handedly manufactured.

By studying the remains of the

host creatures, Alfie figured the larvae could have likely sustained themselves another six months, perhaps as long as a year. Keeping one of the hosts for his own research, he dissected the other three, dropped them into each of the aquariums, unsure of whether the nutrients were essential to the successful growth of the larvae, in addition to the decomposing vegetation and soil he himself had provided. They were so similar to grubs, down to the shining extended buckeye head and protracted limbs, that he assumed they could consume similar nutrients. And so far his theory proved correct. The grubs seemed to be thriving—not one had died—and the pieces of the adult hosts were being devoured as greedily as the roots and vegetation he'd provided. He knew it would be months before any of them developed into pupa, and possibly years before they reached the full imago stage, but he would be patient, and would make sure his research was thorough and held to the highest scientific standard, so when he revealed his findings to the world he would have already achieved the status of leading, if not *exclusive*, expert for the first alien species ever discovered. Books, guest appearances on every major talk show and news program, speaking appearances… he'd have to hire a publicist, a manager, an agent. Perhaps even a movie deal… Why not? His story would be one told throughout the ages. His name would be in every textbook, on the lips of every scientist throughout what remained of the history of mankind.

Sitting on a hard stool at the long counter, Alfie scratched at his unruly beard, watched the aliens thriving in the aquariums, and thought hazily of all the possibilities the future held. All he ever wanted was to be remembered.

To be immortal.

⊠

Alfie worked through the day and into the next. Not eating, not sleeping, driven by thoughts of fame, by the excitement of discovering new life from another world. Finally, his body yielded

to its limitations, his vision grew fuzzy and his hands shook when he tried to write. Eventually he collapsed across the work table, midway through writing a note on the alien's feeding habits.

He slept, but not deeply. There were whispers in his mind, whispers that crawled through his subconscious like a million microscopic lice. They were words… but not any that he could understand. The words were constant, consistent in tone, a steady flow of instruction, of knowledge, being delivered to him in a rhythmic fashion, driven directly into his brain. Whispers, so many whispers… too many… thousands of voices, all speaking at once, all telling him something new. Images pulsed through his mind: sunbaked vistas, hazy pyramids in the distance; an expanse of outer space, colorful galaxies flowing like cotton candy in black ether; a broken army of strange, stalk-like savages, swarming to escape a ravaging enemy attacking from above and beneath; bizarre cities razed to the ground, planets reshaped, civilizations destroyed by an army with countless numbers…

The whispers and images quickened, faster and faster, driving into his head, erupting like a supernova in his mind's eye.

The frantic, overwhelming invading thoughts were *hurting*. His sleeping body began to shake, blood spat from his nose as he groaned and coughed. In the half dream-state (if it was a dream at all), his head felt like it was *swelling*, his brain bursting apart, bubbling with the acid of alien thoughts, visions of unknown worlds no human mind could comprehend. He winced and barked broken denials, as if in a nightmare… fighting the whispers, the *voices*, now, wanting them out of his head… *Stop!* he screamed in his mind. *Please,* he begged, afraid, *please get out… it hurts… you're hurting me… you're HURTING ME! GOD DAMN YOU I SAID STOP!*

With a jerk he woke, raised his head from the cold surface of the laboratory counter on which he'd been dozing with a gasp. His temples pounded viciously, a migraine behind his eyes so sharp and

painful that the room wouldn't come into focus. His stomach flipped and gurgled as if filled with acid, its meager contents wanting, quite badly, to rush up and out. He lurched drunkenly off the stool, his legs immediately buckled and he fell hard, cracked his forehead on the concrete. A stack of notebooks and papers filled with notes, sketches and data collapsed on top of him, scattered across the floor. He moaned, rubbed the butt of one hand into an eye that felt like it might very well explode.

*I need a drink,* he thought, and then, more rationally, *and some fucking food.*

Alfie wasn't sure the last time he'd eaten anything of real substance, didn't think he'd eaten anything at all for days, other than the dregs of a giant bag of greasy chips, whatever beer had remained in his fridge and a couple granola bars he'd dug out of a dusty backpack he'd found tossed into a corner, remains of a former expedition.

He slowly, carefully, got to his feet, one hand resting on the lip of the counter, and let the room sway a moment, then, after a few deep breaths, steady. He wiped a line of drool dangling from his lip, scratched at the week's worth of beard growing like unruly moss just below. *Jesus,* he thought, *I'm a mess. I've got to…*

Then he heard it.

He froze, listening, holding his breath. He didn't move, didn't make a sound, heard only the beating of his heart throbbing in his ears, the sealed room devoid of all other noise… except for… and there it was…

*Scratching.*

He looked at the aquariums, eyes wild.

While he'd slept most of the larvae had transformed, entered the pupa stage. He was shocked. What should have taken weeks, or months even, had happened in mere *days*.

But even so… regardless with the speed with which they were developing, they certainly shouldn't be *moving*, and they most certainly shouldn't be *digging*!

Alfie moved closer to one of the aquariums, saw that the pupae had, miraculously, burrowed deep into the six or so inches of earth, and a few of them were now pushed against the glass, as if trying to continue their path, to go deeper, as was their nature in the adult stage (or at least the nature of their earth sister, the beetle), in order to build a wider, broader nest.

And now pupae were trying to dig through the damned glass. Their undeveloped legs protruded like jagged broken matchsticks from their thick, jelly-like bodies, claws tenaciously flicking blindly against the aquarium sides. To Alfie's relief, the glass was holding.

For now.

The pupae themselves were unlike any he'd ever seen or studied. Each was easily the size of a baby's fist, and had a deep, golden hue pulsing beneath their slick mucilaginous surface. Other than the size, however, they didn't seem to be all that irregular from the earth pupa of a beetle. What *was* strange was the strength and vitality of the aliens. A normal beetle—an earthen beetle—in the pupa stage would be completely stagnant, essentially developing within a chrysalis, awaiting their transformation to full imago before shedding the pupa layer and emerging. But these pupae were active workers. Diggers. The pupae appeared as nothing more than a fat lump of worm with a shining bronze head, complete with new antennae; while the tarsus and claws were emerged, working frantically, the femurs were still hidden beneath the wet golden shell.

As he looked more closely at the undercarriage of one particularly tenacious creature, Alfie could actually see thin scratched lines in the glass where the pupa's claws had grooved the interior surface, as if their claws were made from rock, or diamonds.

The sound of the hard, scratching limbs on glass filled the lab. Combined with his headache, and the nasty dream he'd had, Alfie was suddenly overwhelmed. His heart raced, his breath came in gulps, black spots crowded the corners of his vision. He felt suddenly panicked, perhaps even a little *frightened*. He staggered for the

stairs, wanting suddenly free of the lab, of the strange creatures growing there, of that incessant sound.

Once upstairs he went to the kitchen, all but lunged for the refrigerator. He was out of beer but there was a half-filled bottle of orange juice, a relatively pruned apple, and an unopened packet of cheese slices. He ripped the top off the orange juice and gulped it down, nearly vanquishing the remains in one breath. It wasn't until he lowered it and breathed in deeply that the sharp tang of spoil hit his taste buds. His stomach lurched and gurgled loudly enough to reverberate in the small kitchen. He picked up the apple, prepared to eat it, but thought he may need it for the bugs, so he stuffed it into his pocket and instead unwrapped three or four slices of American cheese and stuffed them into his mouth, the processed dairy turning to mush as he chomped and swallowed it in a dry lump; it sank into his stomach like a ball of grease, slowly digesting in the rancid juice and percolating stomach acid.

He dropped the plastic juice jug to the linoleum, where it clanked, fell over and sloshed out part of its remains onto the floor. He lurched to the bathroom, hoping he wouldn't have to throw it all up, but needing to pee and brush his teeth. His mouth was dry, pasty and sour.

He used the toilet and turned on the faucet to scrub his hands. When he looked into the medicine cabinet's mirror and saw himself, he nearly gasped in shock; there was a brief moment where he, quite literally, did not recognize his own face. His hair was mussed and plastered oddly in places, clumped wildly in others. Facial hair covered his mouth and cheeks and chin in a hazardous tangle; patches of crust and particles of meals long-past clung to the beard like the last survivors of a sinking ship. His eyes were bloodshot, and worse. One eyeball had ruptured a vessel, flooding the sclera with red, giving the right side of his face a monstrous look.

"Damn it," he said, and splashed water over his face, his eyes, his beard

and hair, sloppily grooming himself to a relatively respectable level. "Gotta get it together, man," he told the dripping reflection, and vowed to have a shower and a proper meal before the day was through.

*And what day was it, anyway?* he thought, then shuddered. He'd lost track of time so completely he had no idea. He hadn't followed up with the professor; had left his cell phone, the battery certainly dead, somewhere in the lab. He wondered if his associates, his friends, had grown suspicious of his extended absence without communication. Surely, by now, curiosity would have grown to concern, fictitious dying mother or no. *Have they come to my door? Have they tried? Have they called the police?* He doubted the last. He only had a few friends, and most of them travelled on their own projects, had their own busy schedules.

*Just how long had I been down there?*

The thought of not knowing panicked him slightly, as did his grizzly, wild appearance. "Screw it," he said, and decided a break was in order. A shower, a shave, and a trip out of the house to get himself a solid, cooked meal.

*The bugs will be here when I get back,* he thought, and smiled weakly at his reflection, feeling good—feeling confident—about taking control once more.

He was just about to take off his stinking, sweat-soaked t-shirt, eager to get into the hot spray of a shower, when he heard the muffled sounds of breaking glass.

It came from the lab.

Alfie tore down the stairs and pushed through the reinforced door into the lab space beyond. He slammed it behind him, eyes scanning the aquariums, the tables, the floor. He saw that two of the aquariums had shattered. The other four seemed to be holding, but he could still hear that constant, determined *scratching*. He ran to the aquariums that had broken, saw that heaps of dirt and most of the pupae had spilled out over the table and onto the floor. At first, he went to pick them up, thinking to put the spilled ones into the other aquariums, but as he looked more closely, he noticed that the pupae seemed quite alive and, almost disturbingly so, active. The dozen or so that had dropped to the floor were writhing on the concrete, but not without purpose.

They were *digging*.

And, by the looks of it, making progress.

Alfie could see the frenzied pupae tearing at the concrete floor, deep scratches already evident where two or more seemed to be working—somewhat impossibly, Alfie thought—in unison.

Mesmerized, and more than a little curious, Alfie stepped over to the other aquariums, careful not to accidentally step on the pupae, although a part of him wondered if it was to keep from smashing them or from hurting himself. *Those claws must be razor sharp.*

He picked up the first aquarium, the glass sides vibrating with the efforts of the pupae within scratching for freedom. He tilted it over, let the contents pour down onto the floor—dirt, roots, and golden, wriggling blobs of the pupae all fell into a giant pile, joining the rest. They too, without hesitation, started attacking the floor with their claws, the tibia on each creature a blur of frenetic motion.

Alfie turned over the remaining aquariums, one-by-one, creating a great pile of dirt and alien bugs on the lab floor. He pushed the mortician tables to the side of the room, clearing as much space as he could for the bugs to work, and for his own observation.

He stacked the empty aquariums against a wall, then backed to the doorway, shower and food forgotten,

and slid down to the floor, his back against the door, amazed by the power and tenacity of these creatures that had not even yet reached the imago stage of their lives.

He pulled the shriveled apple from his pocket, thought about taking a bite, and then tossed it overhand into the pile of dirt.

It was immediately devoured.

### 4

The first adult spawned three days later.

The Meketaten, as Alfie had come to refer to the scarab-like creatures, for reasons he didn't wholly understand, had burrowed through the basement floor, the foundation, and into the earth below the house. Alfie hadn't gone down into the tunneled earth

to thoroughly investigate, primarily because he feared the tenacity of the workers (he didn't want his limbs perceived as an obstruction, to be sawed through the way they had torn through concrete, rock and earth). But he had crawled to the edge of the massive crater in his floor, easily big enough to drive a car through, and flashed an industrial flashlight down into the depths the Meketaten had created.

At first, there didn't seem to be a bottom, but then he noticed the deep tunnel that they'd dug curved northward, so that he saw only the tunnel's bend and, not having a powerful enough light to illuminate it, assumed it a bottomless void.

They had gone on to dig multiple tunnels, extending outward from Alfie's property, each wide enough

for a human being to walk through, if slightly hunched over, and who knew how long. He assumed, based on his early study of insect life, that they had built a nest somewhere down there, deep in the belly of the Earth. It was from one of these tunnels he saw the first adult emerge.

It was the most beautiful thing he'd ever seen.

The large creature caught the beam of his light as it climbed up and out into the main sunken area, just below the home's foundation. Alfie had been shining the flashlight downward, trying to count the number of tunnels the Meketaten had created, when the alien scrambled into view. It was a massive thing, long as a small dog, perhaps, and wide as a baby sea tortoise. Its antennae were long and black, tensing and twitching in the depths. The shell was a solid bright gold, shiny and clean as chrome, with three bright green luminescent dots set neatly across, about midway down its shell. The creature had looked up at Alfie, as if sensing him, and immediately skittered up the sloping dirt path toward him, as if anxious to say hello to a new friend.

Alfie panicked, suddenly very afraid of what the fully-adult creature might do to a human, given the strength and cutting ability of the pupa spawn.

He wanted to stand, to run, to regroup. He tried to get his legs under him, but the room swooned and he fell back on his ass with a grunt. *Too weak,* he thought in a panic. His head was pounding to raise the dead, his eye throbbed like it would burst from its socket. He groaned, nearly sobbed at the thought that he'd let himself get this bad, ignore his own needs, the needs of his body. He turned his head, looked back toward the hole.

He watched with wide bloodshot eyes, in fascination and horror, as the creature emerged, first the long

> He was just about to take off his stinking, sweat-soaked t-shirt, eager to get into the hot spray of a shower, when he heard the muffled sounds of breaking glass.
> It came from the lab.

antennae, then the jet-black head, its mouth wet and dripping, eyes shining like burning black suns. It had slick jaws and a monstrous beak. The beak was shaped like jagged teeth.

Alfie let out a terrified squawk and shuffled on has ass back and away from the hole, kicking wildly as he pushed himself to the far wall, his eyes never leaving the emerging creature.

The adult heaved itself easily, nimbly, onto the concrete floor and skittered straight toward Alfie, its sharp legs clicking like tiny pistol shots as it crossed the floor. Terrified, knowing the thing wanted nothing but his insides for a meal, he looked around desperately. The handle of the rock hammer jutted from over the edge of the mortician table he had pushed aside, the one still bearing the vessel these beings had inhabited on their trip through space. Adrenaline and fear fueled his movements and he reached up and snatched the hammer, fingertips brushing the black leather of the handle just as the creature scrambled onto his foot. With a pathetic cry he swung the sharp edge of the hammer down at the thing, putting all his remaining strength and terror behind the blow, hoping to spear it and keep himself alive a little longer.

The hammer hit the golden shell and clanged off without even scratching the surface. The creature didn't, in fact, seem to notice Alfie's effort.

The hammer clanked to the ground as the alien climbed onto his leg, its front legs already gripping one knee like a steel clamp. Alfie tried to kick at it, in vain, he supposed, and the thing—the *Meketaten*—only clambered higher, its hard, sharp claws poking into Alfie's thighs and hips like spears. In trying to pull away from the thing Alfie only managed to slide his body off the wall, his torso flopping to the ground as the creature moved higher, undaunted, before settling heavily on his stomach and heaving chest. Its onyx eyes stared emptily at Alfie's own, its antennae stroking his face with soft, wiping slashes. Alfie couldn't believe the *weight* of the thing. Despite being no bigger than a shoebox, the creature felt

like a cinderblock weighing him down.

Alfie was about to do something—to scream, to fight—when the creature *spoke* to him, its audible voice an inhuman series of squeaks and clicks.

*You are dying,* it said.

Alfie couldn't believe it. The thing was communicating with him… speaking in indecipherable sounds… but he could understand it. *The thing speaks English,* he thought, almost laughing at the idea.

*Not English, Khepri,* it said, reading his thoughts, its jaws working as it hissed and clicked, tendrils of warm liquids sliding from its mouth, wetting Alfie's shirt. *But you CAN understand, because we will it so. You are dying, Khepri. You must not die. It is almost time now.*

The creature stared at Alfie another moment, its glassy black eyes studying him, then turned nimbly and scrambled away, off his body, across the floor, disappearing over the edge of the hole, down into the tunnels, back toward the nest.

Alfie watched it go, his body going limp with relief as it vanished from sight… at which time he promptly, and most thoroughly, passed out.

When he finally came to, groggy and drained, Alfie wasn't sure how much time had passed. He laid face-down on the cool surface of the basement floor, too weak to stand, too tired to do anything but watch the coming-and-going of the now very large quantity of adult Meketaten that clambered in and out of the hole in his basement floor. Unlike the first adult, who had made a point to visit him straightaway, the rest of the scrambling creatures seemed to be completely ignoring Alfie's presence. So he just laid there and gawked at the amazing alien beings and their hectic building pace.

The lab itself was unrecognizable.

They had layered the walls and counters with dirt and dung, smashed through the reinforced door and created the head of an earthen tunnel leading upwards toward his home. The

fluorescent lights still shone, and some counter-edges still protruded through the packed earth, but Alfie felt as if he'd been taken from his home and dropped into a faraway cave on a planet not his own.

As the Meketaten worked, Alfie passed in and out of unconsciousness, wondered absently if his wasted body would be used for food.

During a particularly cognizant moment, he noticed a massive adult emerge from the hole, twice the size of his previous visitor—*my god they're getting bigger,* he thought—and walk toward him. It was long and wide as a wheelbarrow, and Alfie didn't want to even think how heavy it must be. He prayed this one didn't clamber onto his chest, confident it would crush his ribs like toothpicks.

As it got closer, Alfie noticed the giant creature held a large membrane, sagging from its jaws like a veined water balloon, a rubbery-looking sack that wiggled and writhed. A womb with a hundred feisty babies eager to get out.

Alfie's eyes fell closed once more, his exhaustion complete. He watched through a blurred haze as the sack hit the floor, saw the bundle of fresh larvae spill out. The giant creature angled its face down to look directly into Alfie's own, its mouth hissing and clicking, its breath surprising clean and earthy, like the inside of a cave, or the bottom of a new grave.

*There is good news,* Alfie heard, translating the language in his mind somehow. *We have begun mating, Khepri,* it said, all squeals and wet clicks. *The time is near, and you must eat.*

Alfie tried to respond, to question… but could only moan and drool into the dirt-smattered concrete beneath his head. His eyes rolled up into his head, something deep in his brain *popped,* and the last thing Alfie was conscious of happening was the shocking sensation of a strong, stick-like object entering his mouth and pulling his jaw open. His tongue lolled, rubbed against the coarse hairs of the creature's limb.

Something moist and wiggling was shoved into his mouth. The taste was bitter and the mushy, twisting object filled his cheeks, juices running down his throat. He tried to bite, to spit it out, but instead his mouth was gently—firmly—closed, and it took hardly any effort at all to swallow the thing down.

The giant creature's claw opened his mouth once more and another larva was pushed inside. This time Alfie swallowed greedily, then opened his mouth for more.

With the patience of a mother caring for her young, the creature continued the feeding.

### 5

Alfie slept, and dreamed of great things. A boundless golden army that could attack by air, by ground, from *beneath* the ground. Millions strong. A raging storm cloud of creatures, nearly indestructible. Flying sun-fueled warriors the size of tanks—swarms of them.

He was shown visions of destroyed cities, of nations, of every people. The extinction of entire civilizations.

In a state of semi-consciousness that lasted an indefinable period of time, Alfie felt the bustling legs of the creatures—so many creatures—upon him, ripping and stripping away his clothing, tugging at his hair, his face, feeding him, whispering to him, *teaching* him. Their voices filled his mind, spilled their history, and the history of mankind, into his own memories, and he took it all in... he listened.

His mind continued to be bombarded with images, and it was as if he were reliving his own memories. Alfie could see vast sand-filled plains, vistas of wild green forest, vegetative planets with landscapes beyond his ability to fathom, burning landscapes where creatures of fire were laid waste, mountainous vistas, cities of blue metal populated by giant men.

*There are others,* they said.

In his own world, thousands of years ago, a leader was chosen by Earth's Meketaten, the army of Aten, the Sun God. That leader united civilization, demanded their worship, their compliance. It was a new world order. One of peace, of intelligence. One God for all humankind. An end to wars, to tyranny, to terror. He saw a species of giant Meketaten working side-by-side with Earthmen, building impossible structures, beacons to their brethren's own home planet, billions of light years away, where the true Aten resided, the creator of suns, the creator of life. The One God.

These Meketaten, these travelers, had built civilizations before, but man and Earth had failed. And now the time had come to try again, begin the rebirth, start the world over, hope mankind could survive and build, carry the light of the supreme being that humans called Aten, Itzamna, Yahweh, Amun, Shiva, Nugua... too many to count, too many to name.

As the thoughts persisted, some distant part of Alfie could feel the larvae bursting apart inside him, the fluids and alien bacteria from the creatures rushing into his bloodstream, expanding his heart, reshaping his delicate, intricate brain.

His body was lifted, placed by sharp but gentle claws onto the back of a giant creature. He could sense more than see being carried down, down into the depths, toward the nest. His world lifted up and away as he went lower and lower, his fingers dragging in soft dirt as darkness encompassed him completely.

He was set down inside a chamber as vast as Solomon's palace, an entryway to the massive honeycomb of caverns and tunnels already reaching beyond the city, spiraling downward and outward, new catacombs being even now created and filled, reaching even further. His eyes prickled, sharp needling pains shooting through them. He opened them, blinking, and was surprised he could see clearly down in the depths. A duotone yellow showed every crevice of the cavernous fulcrum.

The vast walls crawled with countless golden shells.

He was no longer fed. He was so full now, his body could digest no more. He defecated, his body emptying itself, and the creatures methodically combined it with their own waste, spread out in great piles throughout the cavern. The Meketaten covered Alfie with the waste, then rolled his bloated body, his stomach a giant flexed womb of nutrients pumping through his system, into a great pile of dung. They continued to roll him into a massive ball of dirt and shit, inside which he laid, dormant, at the center of a chrysalis, awaiting transformation.

In the quiet, warm dark, Alfie curled into himself like an unborn child; could hear his heart beating faster, faster. Visions and information was translated into his mind like a hurricane, expanding his brain, physically reshaping his skull into an oblong shape, the parietal plate breaking and pushing backward, stretching skin, reforming into an antenna with which he could communicate with the One God, as well as the other Meketaten; to receive and provide information, relay the will of the great one. Lead them.

As the transformation slowly continued, he felt—numbly, with awareness but no pain—his limbs crack, reshape, lengthen, then quickly heal. Stronger than before. Stronger than bone, than steel.

A thick secretion spilled from his pores, hardened around him, over him. His back broadened, shoulders separated and extended, muscle ripped apart and regrew, sinew sprouting like weeds inside as his skin became shell.

His new mind started to finalize its ultimate form, and the part of him still human wondered if he would fly, if he would swarm with his brothers, his children, and watch the destruction of what mankind had built from high above, caressed by the cool mist of clouds, the warmth of the One God spread across his impenetrable carapace like a guiding hand, the hand of a father.

They will call him Ateuchus, and when he emerged, the new world would begin. His creatures, having created this new man, will scream like locusts, "*See him! See the great one, uniting the earth.*"

And he will rise, burning like the golden sun. ◉

# FEATURED FILM REVIEW

# GOKE: BODY SNATCHER FROM HELL

BY COLLEEN WANGLUND

*Goke: Body Snatcher from Hell*
(Japan, 1968)
Director: Hajime Sato

Many of us are familiar with the low-budget Japanese science fiction/horror films of the 1960s. Dominated by rubber-suited monsters and other weird and scary creatures threatening Tokyo with destruction or in some cases, protecting the city, a good number of these films also shared the popular anti-war theme of post-WWII Japanese movies in general. We all know Godzilla, Mothra, Gamera, and Rodan, monsters that revolutionized the art of Special Effects, especially in regard to miniatures. One particular sci-fi/horror film that really stands out without the use of monsters or miniatures is Hajime Sato's *Kyuketsuki Gokemidoro* (translation: The Gokemidoro Vampire), but is known to English-speaking audiences in the west as *Goke: Body Snatcher from Hell*.

A Japan Air flight takes off from Tokyo into a blood red sky. The passengers include Senator Mano (Eizo Kitamura); arms dealer Tokiyasu (Nobuo Kaneko) and his wife Noriko (Yuko Kusunoki); Mrs. Neal (Kathy Horan (*The Green Slime, 1968*)), an American widow bringing the body of her husband home; Momotake (Kazuo Kato), a psychiatrist; Professor Sagai (Masaya Takhashi), who is a space biologist; a hijacker (Hideo Ko); and a teenage bomber. Not long after take-off, the pilot (Hiroyuki Nishimoto) receives a message that there is a bomb on board and he is instructed to return the plane to the Tokyo airport. To avoid panic, co-pilot, Sugisaka (Teruo Yoshida *(Horrors of Malformed Men, 1969)*), tells the passengers that some classified documents were loaded onto the plane by mistake and he must check the baggage. Fearing being caught, the hijacker (Hideo Ko) points a gun at Sugisaka and orders the pilot to fly the plane to Okinawa.

He then shoots the radio just as it was announcing a UFO spotted over Japan. The plane is hit by a flock of bloody birds and then fired on by the UFO, crashing in a desolate area.

Sugisaka and flight attendant Kuzumi (Tomomi Sato) survey the damage and discover that the pilot and some of the passengers are dead. When they discover that there isn't much food or water, the survivors get angry. The hijacker, thought to be dead, grabs Kuzumi and runs off with her, eventually coming upon the mysterious UFO that fired on the plane. Hypnotized by an unknown force, the hijacker leaves Kuzumi and enters the craft. There we meet the evil alien entity—a mercury-like blob of a vampire called Gokemidoro—who enters the man's head through an inflicted wound, and takes control of his body. Kuzumi is found, unconscious, by Sugisaka who brings her back to the downed plane. The psychiatrist Momotake hypnotizes

Kazumi so she can tell the survivors what happened. The alien/vampire, using the hijacker's body, makes its way to the crash site, looking to feed. The survivors are still at each other's throats, making Gokemidoro's job that much easier. The creature feeds on one survivor after another. It speaks to the survivors, telling them that there are others like him and they are invading the Earth with plans to wipe out humanity.

*Goke: Body Snatcher from Hell* is most definitely low budget, but it's one very cool flick. While in the air, the plane flies into a bright, blood-red sky—a background that was later recreated by Quentin Tarantino in *Kill Bill: Volume 1* (2003) when the Bride is on the plane flying to Japan. *Goke* is saturated in bright, primary colors that initially seem funky but soon become garish, reflecting the mood of the film. When the vampire feeds, its victims' bodies turn a bright shade of blue before turning to dust; there are other scenes that are bathed in bright yellows and oranges.

The characters are a cross-section of some of the worst personalities found in humanity. They are greedy, arrogant, and self-centered, unwilling to help their fellow passengers in light of their dire circumstances. The hijacker and a teenage bomber take actions for no apparent reason other than to make their respective political statements. Momotake, the psychiatrist, revels in the other passengers' selfish behavior as the situation spirals out of control. Senator Mano and the arms dealer Tokiyasu have had illegal dealings, in which Tokiyasu promised to fund Mano's campaign in exchange for Mano getting the committee to accept Tokiyasu's weapons bid, but Mano has no intention of keeping his end of the bargain.

At one point in the film, Mano

suggests using Mrs. Neal as bait to see if the alien is truly a vampire, and the others are perfectly willing to go along with the idea (this bit perhaps touches on underlying discrimination, as Mrs. Neal is not Japanese). He feels that using a foreigner will cause fewer problems later on, if they survive the alien encounter. Most of the passengers use others to protect themselves from the alien vampire, as opposed to trying to kill it. Ultimately they use the young bomber as a sacrifice, hoping to appease the creature. It's a rather

disgusting display of the worst human traits. The only characters worthy of sympathy are the co-pilot Sugisaka and flight attendant Kuzumi. They not only attempt to help the crash survivors, despite the others' behavior, but they are the only ones to show any sort of compassion or faith in humanity (although that faith is sorely misplaced).

The anti-war theme of *Goke: Body Snatcher from Hell* is glaringly evident. The survivors turning on each other in the wake of disaster reflects the

Cold War era of countries turning on each other and posturing with nuclear weapons, threatening the end of civilization as we know it. The final scenes of the film only serve to emphasize the anti-war sentiment. And as with many of the other sci-fi/horror movies coming from Japan at the time, *Goke*'s final scenes remind viewers of the destruction suffered by a country that had nuclear warheads used against it, with devastating results. The American passenger, Mrs. Neal, is another nod to anti-war sentiment. She is on her way to retrieve her husband's body, an American soldier killed in the Vietnam War, which was exploding on the televisions in living rooms everywhere thanks to regular news broadcasts with graphic images of death and destruction. This was something which had never been seen on a nightly basis before.

The end of the film holds quite a twist. Writers Kyuzo Kobayashi and Susumu Takaku and director Hajime Sato leave no doubt as to the hopelessness of the situation their characters find themselves in. *Goke: Body Snatcher from Hell* is one of the bleakest films I've ever seen, which is something I happen to like in horror films. As much as I love the kaiju films of the same era, they always seemed to end on a positive note, stressing faith in humanity's compassion and ability to survive. *Goke* gives barely a hint at redemption for humanity, the only exception being the characters of Kuzumi and Sugisata, and that is why it is so disturbing. Sato was not afraid to bring the savagery of the human race to the big screen in an alien invasion/vampire metaphor. Gruesome, somber, and haunting, it is beautifully filmed and the video and audio effects are stunning, as is the movie's soundtrack which only adds to the film's very cool apocalyptic vibe. ◉

BY BRETT TALLEY

Let's set the scene. Archeologists, stumbling through an unknown jungle, come upon a lost city of great antiquity. Its complexity and size seems beyond the capability of the local peoples, and carved into its sides are ancient glyphs. Their meaning cannot be precisely discerned, but they seem to hint at gods who descended from the stars and built the city. Not only that, but they left a promise to return one day, when the time is right.

Now the question: H.P. Lovecraft story, right? Or an episode of the History Channel's hit show, *Ancient Aliens*? Not an easy question, is it?

If you're not sure of the answer, don't feel bad. The similarities between the Cthulhu mythos and the Ancient Astronaut Theory are so strong as to defy mere coincidence.

That's the position taken at least by Jason Colavito in his scholarly work, *The Cult of Alien Gods: H.P. Lovecraft and Extraterrestrial Pop Culture*. Colavito offers an engrossing, if thoroughly skeptical, history of what has come to be known as the Ancient Alien or Ancient Astronaut Theory. For those unfamiliar with the cable program and the works of theorists like Erich von Däniken and Zecharia Sitchin, the Ancient Alien Theory posits that deep in the shrouded mist of our planet's distant past, Earth was visited by extraterrestrials. The details can vary depending on who's telling the story, but these ETs played a significant role in mankind's development and evolution. Some adherents claim that human beings are a creation of an advanced race whose mastery of genetic engineering allowed them to create homo sapiens out of some lower form of life. Essentially, it's Intelligent Design with aliens instead of God, or the plot of *2001: A Space Odyssey*.

That's the most extreme view. The slightly less all-encompassing tack—though still pretty extreme in and of itself—is that these creatures

Image: Leo Blanchette/Shutterstock.com

found primitive man at some very early stage of civilization. Following the maxim that any sufficiently advanced technology appears to be magic, à la Robert Heinlein, these primitive peoples took alien visitors for gods, basing all of the world's mythologies on their visitations. As a corollary, the aliens acted in the role of Prometheus, giving unto early man knowledge that should have taken centuries or even thousands of years to develop. In this way, aliens were directly responsible for the construction of many of the world's wonders. And when they left, they promised that one day they would return.

That's the Ancient Alien Theory in a nutshell, and Colavito's recitation of it adds little to what we already know. But Colavito goes well beyond simply describing the views of others. Instead, he digs beneath those views to find their underpinnings, developing a fascinating theory of his own, particularly for any fan of weird fiction. The Ancient Alien Theory isn't grounded in archeological anomalies or seemingly impossible cities or monuments. For Colavito, the entire Ancient Alien craze has none other than H.P. Lovecraft to thank for its creation.

I'll let you read Colavito's book and examine the evidence, but I'll tell you that it is quite convincing. Nevertheless, his is a bold claim, and an ironic one, too. Lovecraft was, if nothing else, a dedicated materialist and rationalist. The kind of pseudoscience that the Ancient Alien Theory relies on would have struck him as nothing less than silly. Mystical dream quests, ancient beings from the stars, and tomes of magical incantations were useful plot devices for fiction, but to believe they could be real? Not Lovecraft.

But while Lovecraft might have scoffed at the claims of Giorgio Tsoukalos were he alive today, we can be sure they would find their way into his fiction. Whatever the truth of Colavito's thesis and whatever one believes about the truth or absurdity of the Ancient Alien Theory, there can be little doubt that Lovecraft and weird fiction in general have long capitalized on the notion that there is something beyond our world and that at some point we have been visited

But while Lovecraft might have scoffed at the claims of Giorgio Tsoukalos were he alive today, we can be sure they would find their way into his fiction. Whatever the truth of Colavito's thesis and whatever one believes about the truth or absurdity of the Ancient Alien Theory, there can be little doubt that Lovecraft and weird fiction in general have long capitalized on the notion that there is something beyond our world and that at some point we have been visited by creatures from beyond the stars.

by creatures from beyond the stars. One of the most famous passages from Lovecraft's seminal "The Call of Cthulhu" so perfectly encapsulates the Ancient Astronaut Theory that it is little wonder Colavito and others trace that theory back to Lovecraft:

> Old Castro remembered bits of hideous legend that paled the speculations of theosophists and made man and the world seem recent and transient indeed. There had been aeons when other Things ruled on the earth, and They had had great cities. Remains of Them, he said the deathless Chinamen had told him, were still to be found as Cyclopean stones on islands in the Pacific. They all died vast epochs of time before men came, but there were arts which could revive Them when the stars had come round again to the right positions in the cycle of eternity. They had, indeed, come themselves from the stars, and brought Their images with Them.

Lovecraft goes on to speak of great Cthulhu himself, explaining that he had also come from the stars, to rule the earth. But at some point in the distant past, things went wrong. Lovecraft never explains how or why the Great Old Ones lost dominion over the earth, but lose it they did. Locked in the dark places of this world, on the highest mountains and

in the deepest canyons, or simply far beneath the waves, they await the moment of their return.

This is the central idea at the heart of all of Lovecraft's best and most sophisticated stories. Not only ancient visits, but something left behind. Something that could invade the dreams of men, that defied the settled expectations of life, the truth of which would drive men mad were it known. He revisits this motif again and again, from "The Nameless City" to "The Shadow out of Time." And always the promise of return.

The casual observer might think that it is on this point of "return" where Lovecraft and the Ancient Alien Theorists would go their separate ways. After all, the former believe extraterrestrials to be benevolent beings, while the Great Old Ones of Lovecraft care nothing for mankind and will likely wipe us from the face of the earth as an afterthought. This view is widely accepted dogma by Lovecraft aficionados, but interestingly, that's not exactly how Lovecraft paints it. In "The Call of Cthulhu," he writes of the Great Old Ones return,

> That cult would never die till the stars came right again, and the secret priests would take great Cthulhu from His tomb to revive His subjects and resume His rule of earth. The time would be easy to know, for then mankind would have become as the Great Old

> Ones; free and wild and beyond good and evil, with laws and morals thrown aside and all men shouting and killing and reveling in joy. Then the liberated Old Ones would teach them new ways to shout and kill and revel and enjoy themselves, and all the earth would flame with a holocaust of ecstasy and freedom. Meanwhile the cult, by appropriate rites, must keep alive the memory of those ancient ways and shadow forth the prophecy of their return.

That's actually not all that different from what Ancient Alien Theorists claim will happen when the extraterrestrials return. It's darker and more violent—Lovecraft was a horror writer after all—but let's break down the basic components. The ETs won't return until mankind becomes like them, perhaps achieving a technological level where they would be viewed as simply more advanced rather than gods. They will then teach mankind new things that could not have been imagined, ushering in a new age.

Call it fact or accept it as fiction, but it's hard not to see the connections. And one wonders why mankind is so drawn to this notion of an outside power, meddling in our affairs, bringing us towards the light, or threatening our destruction. Maybe Lovecraft was more right than he ever could have known. ⊙

LITTLE

# WING

## BY JEFFREY THOMAS

### 1: Mr. Dolor

"Show me the fairy."

Osman Ginko stepped back to let the new arrival enter the "safe" apartment he had arranged to use for this transaction. He turned from the door and started down a hallway toward the last of the unoccupied flat's three bedrooms. He wouldn't have turned his back on this guest, who went by the name Mr. Dolor, had Ginko's partner O'lz not been present to follow after Mr. Dolor in turn. O'lz was a female KeeZee, an odd albino specimen, seven feet tall as was the norm but the film of flesh sucked tight to her fearsome-jawed head was clear instead of gray-black, her veins showing vividly through it. Her dreadlocks were white instead of black, her three tiny eyes pink instead of black. She never spoke; she was wont to let her assault engine, currently gripped in both fists, handle any important communication.

The walls of the hallway, and its floor and ceiling—as in every room of the apartment, in fact—were double sheets of clear plastic. Sandwiched between them was an orange gel with a subtle, constant glow. A species of black worm, the largest specimens over a foot long, had once tunneled through this nourishing gel, not serving any practical purpose but just part of the decor. However, the thousands of worms had long since all sickened and died, their shriveled carcasses entombed in the mazes of burrows they had made. Before Mr. Dolor's arrival, gesturing at one wall, Ginko had joked to O'lz, "This will be Punktown one day… when we've all killed each other off."

Punktown was the nickname of this city, and Punktowners were ravenously hungry, as these worms had been.

A long nail was driven into the closed door to the third bedroom, and from it hung two military-style gas masks with goggles. Ginko took them down and passed one to Mr. Dolor, saying, "Here—put this on."

Mr. Dolor hesitated, then handed his mask back. "I need to know what this is like, firsthand."

"It's like a lot," warned Ginko.

"Okay," said Mr. Dolor. "I should hope so." He jerked his chin at the KeeZee. "What about her?"

"Not all races are affected."

"I see." Now Dolor nodded at the door. "Open it."

"As you like." Ginko hung Dolor's mask by its strap again, fitted his own mask onto his head, then opened the door and led his guest inside.

A kitchen table stood in the room's center, the only piece of furniture in the apartment at this time. Upon it rested a large metal cylinder, which Ginko went to stand beside. Dolor stopped at its foot. "Ready?" asked Ginko.

"Go," said Dolor, glancing from one to the other of the two windows in the room. Their panes had been adjusted to a full black tint for privacy. He realized this was bound to be embarrassing.

Ginko touched a key on the cylinder's side, and its topmost portion slid away, curved down into the lower portion. Dolor leaned forward for a better look at its contents, even as Ginko pressed another key that set two fans in the floor of the cylinder to spinning, wafting a soft breeze up into Dolor's face... bringing with it an odd musty smell, brown and aged in character, like crispy autumn leaves, a squashed forest mushroom, a pile of old newspapers, but with something else in the mix: a muskiness that was not decay, that had resisted decay. A scent that was vital and immediate... inexplicably universal and eternal.

Resting in the little coffin was an odd, anthropomorphic figure, small as a child. Mummified, desiccated, its skeletal frame seemingly spray-painted with a thin coating of skin. Its flesh was gray, its half-open eyes intact and entirely black, its dark lips withered away from a crazed grin of yellow teeth. Its forehead head sloped back radically, the rear of the elongated skull tapering almost to a point. Crossed upon its chest were two wings, now dry parchments but once supple membranes growing down from the lower arms to the outsides of the legs.

Osman Ginko—purveyor of dubious and ill-gotten rarities, skilled at relating their histories and virtues—explained, "The Fahleet have been extinct for over a hundred years. They were a primitive tribe on Kali—a peaceful people overall, from all accounts—but the Kalians saw them as offensive savages, if not outright demons because of their wings, so they systematically wiped them out over the years. You know the Kalians.

Funny, though, how they used parts of their bodies as icons. Wind chimes and flutes made out of their hollow bones. Plenty of old books, even copies of their holy book the Fizala, used Fahleet wing leather for their covers. Not that they really flew... they glided."

"Ohh," said Dolor, but it didn't sound like an acknowledgement of Ginko's informative discourse. It sounded like the start of a moan. He hadn't taken his eyes off the mummy. The folded wings left a gap between them that revealed the long-dead entity to have been a female.

"And then," Ginko went on, watching the man through his goggles, "there were the bodies that were preserved in whole, like this one."

"I can picture them," Dolor said dreamily, as if speaking under hypnosis. "I can see them clearly... like a vid in my head. They built houses up in the trees... higher and higher up, in taller and taller trees, as the Kalians worked to exterminate them."

"Yes," Ginko confirmed.

"They protected their young in their shelters, taught them their language. I can hear it!" Dolor shivered. "They glided from tree to tree gathering fruit. Sometimes, those that lived close to the coastline soared for hours on the ocean breezes, dipping down to snatch fish from the water—" his speech grew more rapid, more animated "—and they clung to the cliff faces and the trees and the females flapped their wings and emitted their pheromones... their intoxicating musk... drivingpotentialmatescrazythemalesfoughtover-thewomenintheairandplummetedto-theirdeathstilldruggedfrenziedbythe-muskanduuuuuhhhhh!"

Dolor tried to scramble up onto the table, up onto the cylinder, but the KeeZee O'lz had been ready for this. Quickly passing her gun to Ginko, she seized the man from behind in a bear hug and pulled him backwards, held him tightly as he squirmed and kicked his legs in the air. He let out a long, howling cry of frustrated lust. Dolor had had the hair on his head and eyebrows removed and replaced with silvery metal bristles, so these scraped

at O'lz through her black jumpsuit, but it didn't faze her. She backed off further, and Ginko set aside the assault engine, went to the table, and turned off the two fans inside the cylinder. Its cover hissed back into place.

Gradually, after a drawn-out and violent shudder of spontaneous orgasm, Dolor went limp in O'lz's arms. Gently, like a mother who had calmed her child's tantrum, she set him down on his feet and released him.

He tottered a little but caught himself, looking down self-consciously at his still tented trousers. He had never experienced a climax of such intensity.

Still panting, Mr. Dolor looked up at Ginko with a semblance of his former professional demeanor and said, "I'll take it."

### 2: Valentin

Marcel Valentin had been a popular vid actor in Punktown for decades, and actors of his level of fame acquired a kind of immortality, but in his personal life he had endeavored to make that immortality a more literal thing. He was one-hundred-and-nine years old. Twenty-five years ago, when surgical procedures and an increasing measure of cybernetics had no longer been able to convincingly keep age at bay (more so on the inside than the outside), he had had himself cloned and his recorded memories transferred into this new body. His new body had been progressed only to the age of forty-two, when his flame had burned its brightest, and his original body had been incinerated. This procedure had been accomplished for him by the Neptune Teeb crime syndy, because cloning of private citizens (as opposed to clones used for labor and the military) was illegal.

But early this year, when his forty-two-year-old body had reached the age of sixty-seven, he decided to have himself cloned a second time. He had this new vehicle for his memories advanced only to the age of twenty-nine, the age he had been when his star had first risen. The former clone was scrubbed of its memories (he couldn't share his life with another him, could he?) but he kept it around—in cryogenic storage at his vacation home down south in the Outback Colony—in case he ever wanted to produce a dead version of himself later, and go on with his life under a new identity. After all, at one-hundred-and-nine years old, he had to reluctantly admit his long vid career was at an end. Short of computer trickery, how could he explain away his youthfulness in the public eye now, but to admit to illegal activities?

Ah, but it was a bittersweet thing, an aching tease, to be so young and handsome again, and yet not be able to play the rugged leading men, the tough-guy forcers, the violent gangsters he had specialized in. (Neptune Teeb himself had told Valentin he was a big fan.)

He tried to take his mind off this yearning for the past by indulging in activities that, within his Beaumonde Square penthouse, were shielded from the public eye. But a man of his wealth and long years had partaken of many varieties of pleasure. It could be a challenge devising or discovering more. That was one of the tasks he entrusted to his combination personal assistant, manservant, and bodyguard, Mr. Dolor.

Not that Mr. Dolor was his only servant. Recently he had hired a Sinanese woman as his housecleaner. He had had a couple of Sinanese lovers before; one a woman, one a ladyboy. Both had been beautiful. Like all Sinanese, who hailed from the world Sinan in a coexistent dimension, his housekeeper Lhi was on the short side, with long black hair and pale blue skin. She was in her late twenties, he figured, and a little meatier than his past lovers, but still sufficiently attractive. Only a week into her employment, he had cornered her one day in the guest bedroom while she was cleaning and pressed himself upon her. She had given in, after initial inarticulate protests (her English was limited) and a few tears, and he had tucked a hundred munit bill into her hand afterwards, stroking that long hair soothingly and encouraging her to go buy herself something nice when it was time to go home.

A Sinanese man, also with limited English skills, picked her up in a hovercar at street level every evening. Lhi had told Valentin once the man was her sister. Valentin had laughed. Lhi and her cutely skewed (if occasionally exasperating) English.

Now, whenever he was hungry and he was too lazy to have Dolor summon here a professional working girl or boy—human, otherworlder, or mutant—he simply took Lhi again. Their second time, she had held her hand out to him afterwards, and held him with a stern gaze. Ah, the mercenary little bitch! he thought. But he always gave her the hundred munits, presumably to share with her "sister."

Lhi was presently down in the kitchen, tidying up after dinner, soon to finish for the evening. Valentin and Mr. Dolor were down the hall in the penthouse's playroom. Dolor had just finished setting up the item he had acquired that morning. The "fairy," as it had been called.

The cylinder stood against one wall, tilted but held in place by a frame Dolor had improvised, the capsule's lid still in place. Opposite this silvery coffin was the playroom's bed, its mattress fitted with a sheet of bioengineered living human skin. The bed already had wrist and ankle restraints.

Valentin was not self-conscious about disrobing in front of Mr. Dolor. Mr. Dolor had seen it all. When Valentin had stretched out on his back on the bed and extended his extremities to its four corners, Dolor secured the restraints. Along with the fairy in its receptacle, Osman Ginko had given Dolor the two gas masks. Unlike his first encounter with the mummified Fahleet, Dolor was wearing one of those masks now.

"Butterflies and zebras and moonbeams," Valentin said, smiling, as he watched Dolor strap his left ankle. His again-youthful manhood was already stirring from its sleep. "Is that what I'm going to see, Mr. Dolor?"

"Excuse me, sir?" The gas mask with its blank lenses for eyes lifted quizzically.

"Nothing."

When Valentin was pinned in place, his body a muscular white X, Dolor turned to the cylinder. He touched a key on its side, and its cover slid aside with a whisper.

Valentin strained to lift his head to look upon his acquisition. "Jee-sus," he said, "is that thing hideous." But in anticipation of the fairy's arrival, he had watched old vids of the Fahleet in life, copulating in trees, the females clinging to rough bark while the males mounted them. In life, the nude little beings with their odd gliding webs had been decidedly more enticing.

Dolor pressed a second key, and then stood aside, as fans within the cylinder blew toward Valentin an unseen, microscopic pollen... not made less potent by the being's decay, but perhaps even fermented to a greater headiness. Tiny motes of the Fahleet itself were borne along, entering Valentin's body through his nostrils and greedily gulping mouth.

"Ohhh, man," he said, his head still lifted from the living skin of the bed as he kept his eyes trained on the fairy's own half-closed/half-opened black eyes. "Did you see this, Mr. Dolor?"

"Tell me what you see, sir," said Dolor with his glinting metal hair.

"I can see them! It's like I'm looking through the eyes of one of them! I'm flying, man... I'm flying." He laughed drunkenly, astonished, delighted. "I'm flying over the ocean, Mr. Dolor—I can see my shadow below me on the water! Oh my God... I'm following a smell... an incredible, heavenly scent. A heaven-sent scent!" He laughed again, wildly.

Wheeling on high, soaring like a kite on the ocean updrafts, Valentin looked toward a wall of rugged white cliffs and spotted the source of the intoxicating aroma. A female, clinging to the chalky rock and flapping her gliding membranes with languorous, sensuous movements. Somehow, he knew, it was this female... the one in this very room with him.

Valentin swooped down toward her... closer... closer... alighted upon her back. In this vision, this memory, he penetrated her and she threw back her long pointed head and let out an ululating cry of pleasure.

Valentin jerked his wrists against their bonds. Tendons showed hard in his neck. "Mr. Dolor!" he rasped through gritted teeth. "Oh God, Mr. Dolor... unstrap me! Hurry!"

"Sir," Dolor said calmly through his muffling mask. "Remember, you yourself told me not to allow you to damage the fairy."

"I need her! I need her!"

"I'm sorry, sir, I must follow your orders."

Valentin turned on his assistant a look of rage that even the most bloodthirsty gangster he had ever portrayed, the most righteous forcer vowing vengeance over the body of his slain partner, had never evinced. "Go get me that girl downstairs—quickly!"

"Lhi?"

"Who the blast do you think I mean?" Valentin screeched. "Give her five hundred munits, if you have to, but get her up here!"

Dolor left the room, and though Valentin squeezed his eyes tightly shut to hold off from climaxing before his assistant could return with his housekeeper, it did nothing to cut off the ancient memories he relived as the pair of Fahleets—vainly, as it turned out—strove amorously to perpetuate their species.

Only a minute later, however, Dolor returned, holding a confused looking Lhi by the arm. Her eyes widened at the sight of her employer naked upon the playroom bed.

Valentin opened his eyes, saw her there, and grinned... his great rictus, trembling like a drawn bow, rather like that on the mummy's own face. To Dolor, he said, "Now unstrap me." Then, to Lhi, he instructed, "Take a deep breath, sweetness."

### 3: Yue

Having brought his secondhand hovercar alongside the curb in front of the looming Beaumonde Square apartment tower, Yue opened the passenger's side door when he saw his sister emerging from the building's revolving front door. It wasn't until she bent down and slipped in beside him, however, that he noticed her disheveled hair, hanging across her face, the suction bruises spotting her throat, the tears capping her eyes.

In their native Sinanese tongue, he snarled, "What did he do to you?"

Lhi had never dared tell her brother about how her employer had seduced her. She had told Yue the bonus money she shared with him was tips for her conventional work. This time, though, with the last of her monumental orgasm still echoing through the channels of her body—a tremor she felt sure he could sense—and the smell of sex strong in this enclosed space, she knew she could no longer deceive him. All she could say, in a small gasping voice, was, "Please take me home."

"Did he dishonor you, sister?" Yue demanded.

"Please, Yue... take me home."

Yue looked at her, hard. In certain light, the black Sinanese eye seemed to reflect a red light. His eyes flashed red now. Yue had done bad things in order to bring his sister to what he had hoped would be a better life in this dimension, on this world Oasis, in this city originally called Paxton, created by Earth colonists generations ago. He had sacrificed, he had compromised his integrity, he had even killed (unbeknownst to her) for his younger sister's sake.

He looked through the windshield, no longer pressing her, and started the car forward again. But he circled around to the entrance to the tower's subterranean parking lot.

"Please, Yue, don't," his sister pleaded.

His jaw thrust forward, his body filled with a vibration like but unlike the vibration that shimmered in Lhi's body, he disregarded her pleas, until finally she lapsed into respectful, fatalistic silence.

Though she was an independent worker, not one of the building's official cleaning staff, Valentin had arranged for Lhi to have access to the service elevator at the rear of the building. She and her brother rode in this now, up to the top of the building. During this ascent, Yue continuously muttered the worst of profanity and curses under his breath. For her part, Lhi kept her eyes downcast and fought the urge to vomit.

They walked to the door of Marcel Valentin's penthouse apartment, and Lhi whispered one last time, "Please." Yue ignored her and rang the buzzer.

In the door's vidplate appeared the head of Mr. Dolor, topped with its sparkling metal bristles. "Oh, hello, Lhi. Did you forget something?"

"She forgot pocketbook," Yue said tersely.

They heard the hard clack of the door unbolting, and then it slid open with a hiss.

Yue had a handgun, held down by his thigh. It was not unusual that he owned a handgun; this was Punktown. Yue also had the instincts of a fighter, and knew that Mr. Dolor was not someone to point a gun at to threaten and question. Mr. Dolor would no doubt have a gun of his own. Mr. Dolor would doubtlessly have done his own bad things; it was his job to do bad things. So, Yue pointed the gun at him and simply pulled the trigger.

Yue shot Mr. Dolor in the cheek and jaw and neck and Lhi cried out and squeezed her eyes shut, but as Mr. Dolor fell back to splay on the floor with his limbs flung out in an X, Yue dragged his sister into the apartment and hit the button to close the door behind them.

"What the hell was that?" they heard a voice call from deeper in the apartment. "Mr. Dolor? Mr. Dolor?"

"Call to him!" Yue hissed to his sister.

"Yue!"

"Do it!"

"Mr. Valentin?" Lhi called out. "It is Lhi!"

Around the corner of a doorway, Marcel Valentin leaned his upper body out and said, "Lhi? What were those sounds?" And then he saw Yue take a step forward, once more lifting his pistol. Valentin ducked back with a shriek that none of the tough forcers and gangsters he had played would ever have uttered. Two shots from Yue's

pistol chewed into the doorframe, and then Yue broke into a run and lunged through the threshold.

At the end of a long hallway lined with holographic movie posters he saw Valentin, dressed in a beautifully embroidered silk Ramon robe, about to duck through another doorway. Yue fired two more shots. He heard Valentin scream again shrilly, and the man slammed up against the wall at the hallway's terminus, but he still managed to plunge awkwardly through the open doorway. For his part, Yue was reluctant to exhaust his gun's ammo until he was closer, his target more assured.

"What you do my sister, you fuck?" he shouted, stalking down the hallway with Lhi scrunched down behind him. "Huh? You disgrace my sister like animal?"

Just a few steps before Yue reached the doorway, a more expensive gun than his own was thrust out and Valentin blindly fired several short, red streaks of energy instead of solid bullets. They left smoking black holes in the hallway's left-hand wall, but struck neither of the Sinanese siblings.

Yue ducked down a bit, mindful to keep Lhi shielded behind him, and blasted off three more rounds into the room beyond. He heard a kind of oomph, then the thump of a heavy object striking the floor.

Cautiously, Yue leaned closer to peek into the room, ready to fire his last rounds. He saw it wasn't necessary. Though somewhere down south, unknown to anyone alive, an older version of the actor Marcel Valentin lay mindlessly alive in a stasis chamber, this incarnation of him was dead, with two holes drilled into the V of chest exposed by his robe. He had learned little, it would seem, from the countless gun battles he had participated in during his vids.

The floor upon which he lay was that of the playroom, dominated by the bed with its sheet of living skin and its restraining straps... and facing that, leaning in a kind of support frame, an odd metal capsule large enough to contain a child.

"The thing is in that," Lhi said, pointing.

"What thing?" Yue asked.

"The body of a dead person... or animal... I don't know. Not an Earther, not Sinanese. It has wings, and it has some kind of magic that takes over your mind with visions."

Yue took a step toward the metal cylinder but Lhi cried, "No!" Grabbed onto his arm. She didn't want to tell him how terrible that magic was. That if he opened the cylinder, released the spell bottled up inside, Yue would disgrace his sister himself... and she would enjoy it. She could never tell him how she had enjoyed what Valentin had done to her, enjoyed it beyond any physical experience she had ever known.

"Did this monster kill the person inside?"

"No... it has been dead for many years."

Yue looked at the bed, the straps, then at his sister. He didn't want to ask her to confirm what he envisioned. Instead he said, "We should take this poor being and remove it from here, to be buried properly or burned, so no one like that decadent fiend will abuse its magic again."

"But we mustn't open it, ever!" Lhi implored.

"We won't take any money, any of his valuables," Yue mused aloud, glancing around him. "I don't want to poison my future, and damn my soul. But this relic is coming with us."

Tucking his gun into his rear

waistband, Yue went to the cylinder and lifted it into his arms. He had thought he might need his sister to help him carry it, but the metal was light and so, apparently, were the capsule's contents.

Lhi preceded him back the way they had come, careful to keep her eyes off the body of Mr. Dolor, in its growing pool of blood, on their way to the door.

They rode the service elevator down to the underground parking lot, and Yue placed the cylinder in the trunk of his hovercar.

"The forcers will be looking for us, I'm sure of it," Lhi fretted as she climbed back into the passenger's seat. "I'm sure there are security vids they will look at."

"Let the forcers look for us," Yue said, starting up the vehicle, causing it to rise several feet into the air. "Forcers have looked for me before, here and back home. This city is big. We are unimportant in its eyes. We will disappear." He blew across his upturned palm, as if to disperse some unseen dust.

### 4: Mhin

Some months back Yue and Lhi had rented an apartment on the third floor of a small brick building of pre-colonial Choom origin—the Choom being the native people of Oasis—on Forma Street. The ground floor was occupied by an apothecary run by Yue's friend, and landlord, Mhin. Mhin was thickly built and big-bellied for a Sinanese, but on their world this was a matter of pride; it indicated one was well-fed, and hence comfortable financially. He had lost an eye and scarred half his face in an explosion back on Sinan, while mixing a volatile potion, and now wore a tubular optical device in that socket which gave him enhanced vision almost on the level of the tendril-eyed Tikkihotto race.

Yue had sent Lhi upstairs to hurriedly pack what she needed to bring with them, while Yue and Mhin talked in the latter's workshop at the rear of his store. Without getting into his sister's humiliation, Yue explained to his friend that they were in trouble and had to pull up roots fast.

"Brother," Yue said in their language, "it shames me to ask you, but can you lend me some money? A thousand munits, maybe? You know I'll repay you when I can." He didn't mention the five hundred munits he already had on him. Lhi had pushed the bills into his hand before they'd left the car, without being able to meet her brother's eyes.

"Can't you tell me what is wrong?" Mhin asked.

"It has to do with Lhi's employer. The vid star. You'll see it on the news. And I took something from him, that I would like to dispose of properly. The body of some strange being, Lhi tells me, with magical properties. I don't want to be caught with it, and I would hate to bury it in some filthy abandoned lot in this city, but I don't want to just throw it into a trash zapper. Do you have anything like an incinerator in the basement?"

"Only the trash zapper out back. You say magical properties? How so?" Mhin, less superstitious than his friend, did not believe in magic, despite the potions he sold in his shop. He considered himself a scientist.

"She said breathing in the atmosphere of this being infects the mind… brings visions. It's a small mummy of some kind, with wings."

"Where is it now?"

"In a container, in the trunk of my car."

"Bring it to me."

"Aren't you afraid to be infected?"

From a hook on the wall beside him, Mhin took down a mask he wore when mixing chemicals and ingredients that were best not inhaled freely. "I'll take precautions."

Yue carried the cylinder into the shop through its back entrance, out of the view of Forma Street's traffic and pedestrians, and laid it on Mhin's work table. Mhin told Yue to go upstairs and help Lhi pack while he examined the capsule's occupant.

Alone, Mhin easily found the means by which to open the little coffin's cover, and when confronted by the withered entity inside he said, "Well… and just who are you, old thing?"

He took a picture of the diminutive gray figure with his wrist comp, then ran a query on the net. He came up with a result immediately… and he read about the race called the Fahleet, long exterminated by the predominant race on Kali.

He read of the pheromones the females emitted to attract males during the season of mating, when males would be so driven to a frenzy that they might battle to the death over the object of their desire. But this shriveled corpse, its juices all drained, still emanated these compounds?

Mhin used a scalpel to scrape some dry flakes of skin from one of the mummy's wing-like gliding membranes, and deposited the sample into a scanner. He pored over the results, rubbing his chin with a gloved hand. Turning back to face the body, he studied its face through various different filters and magnifications of his optical device. Under one such filter, its half-lidded obsidian eyes seems to twinkle at him with myriad restless light specks, a constellation of twitching stars not fixed right in the firmament, and he shuddered. As if some mysterious vestige of life still imbued this creature. Who could say? Maybe magic was just science he hadn't yet encountered.

When Yue came back downstairs and cautiously poked his head into the workshop, to find Mhin had sealed the container again, Mhin gestured for him to enter and said, "You had better get as far from this neighborhood as you can. Maybe even leave the city, go to Miniosis or the Outback Colony, if you can. Here." He produced an unlocked cash box, and from it counted out three thousand munits in bills. He handed these to the other blue-skinned man. "This is not a loan. Take your sister away from here."

Yue wagged his head in awe, staring at the bills, then shoved them into his pocket and said, "I am forever in your debt, brother."

"Listen, don't worry about this thing." He motioned toward the cylinder behind him. "I'll deal with it."

"You will? Thank you, Mhin. But

please… don't just toss it into a zapper where trash is burned. Or, if you have no choice, at least say some prayers over it."

"I promise, I will say prayers," Mhin said. "Don't worry… I'll dispose of the body."

It was not entirely a lie.

### 5: Ginko

There had been no security cameras in the home of Marcel Valentin. Osman Ginko imagined the actor had wanted no record of his activities to be blackmailed with. There had, though, been security cameras in the halls of the building which housed Valentin's penthouse, and they showed a Sinanese woman who had been in his employ leaving his apartment in the company of a Sinanese man who may have been her husband or boyfriend, this man carrying a metal cylinder in his arms. What the cylinder had contained, however, the forcers did not know. An inventory of Valentin's belongings was still being assembled, a difficult process with his assistant having been murdered along with him.

Ginko had his fingers on the pulse of Punktown, so he could gauge its desires, its needs. He was familiar with neighborhoods dominated by this or that race of otherworlders, where rare and exotic curiosities could be found.

He had been to the Sinanese apothecary on Forma Street numerous times in the past. He knew the proprietor by name. Mhin was not alarmed to see Ginko step through the front door of his shop in the presence of the towering albino KeeZee female. "Ah, my friends!" he exclaimed. "Would you care for some tea?"

"Please, Mhin—thank you," said Ginko.

Ginko's gaze roved over the shelves all around him, their surfaces crammed full with tiny labeled bottles and sealed baggies. These held powders of every color and consistency, derived from minerals and plants and animals, often in combination. Some jars contained loose leaves and twigs, insects, the dehydrated bodies of tiny lizards.

Preserved in jars of fluid were larval benders. A creature native to Sinan, an adult bender would present itself as a jellyfish as large as a parachute, drifting upon air currents, the dangling tendrils of which delivered a poison that—if it didn't prove fatal—was said to bring on precognitive visions.

Mhin came back with their tea, and the three of them sat at a small table off to one side, while a younger Sinanese man took over at the counter to tend to an old Choom woman seeking some medicinal herbs.

"What can I do for you today, my friend?" Mhin asked.

"I'm helping a client of mine, an important businessman, prepare for a grand party at his home," Ginko explained. "He seeks entertainments of a novel character."

"Your specialty, of course!"

Taking in both men with her three pink eyes, O'lz extended a clear tubular tongue from between her bony, fang-filled jaws and used it to suck at her tea.

"Substances," Ginko went on, "with unique properties he may not have experienced before."

Mhin swept his arm toward the shelf containing jars of pickled benders. "Then might I recommend?"

"Perhaps, perhaps, but I had another thing in mind, specifically. Have your ever come into possession of the body of a race called the Fahleet? They are extinct, now, but were originally to be found on Kali."

Ginko could tell from the way the Sinanese man's face tightened up and his one eye turned wary that his instincts had been correct. "A race called…?"

"My friend," Ginko said in a lower voice, hunching forward, "you know me. I'm not an informer for the forcers. Word on the street—"

"There can't have been any word on the street. Not yet."

"My intuition, then, is that you possess a body. I'd like to purchase it from you."

"I have no body of a Fahleet," Mhin replied. He hesitated, but Ginko saw the hesitation pass. After all, they had done business many times, and the

very point of coming into possession of unique materials was to provide them to his customers. He continued, "What I have, however, is the powdered essence of a Fahleet."

"I see," said Ginko, only somewhat disappointed. He would not ask the man how he had come by this substance; it wasn't actually important now that it was established he was in possession of it. "And it serves as a potent aphrodisiac, as I understand?"

"Most effective," Mhin said solemnly.

"And how does one administer this essence?"

"I would recommend sniffing a mere pinch from the palm, or snorting a line of it from a mirror."

"And have you tried this substance yourself?"

The ever observant Osman Ginko noted that Mhin couldn't prevent himself from glancing guiltily at the young male assistant who at that moment was giving the old Choom woman her change. "I have sampled it. It is an aphrodisiac like no other."

"I think this is exactly the kind of thing my client would be interested in," Ginko said.

"Then I'll show you."

Mhin took Ginko and O'lz to his workshop in the back of the store, and here he bent down to pull out a large drawer from a wall into which set rows and rows of labeled drawers. "How many jars of this essence might you desire?" Mhin asked. "I'll caution you that the material is very concentrated, very powerful in small doses."

Ginko stepped closer to look down into the drawer, at two dozen small bottles into which were dispersed the crushed and powdered remnants of a long-dead fairy.

"Just one jar today, my friend, now that I know you have this," said Osman Ginko, reaching for his wallet.

But he was certain he would be back for more in the future. Punktown was, after all, a city of ceaseless and prodigious appetite. ◐

# BLIGHT

## BY PETER TIERYAS

They call them space slugs. They're big, slimy, and taste kind of like scallops if you put enough sauce on them. Problem is there's never enough sauce.

※

I'm sleeping when I first hear the Crash. I think it's an earthquake because my apartment shakes so much, but the rumbling continues long after the tremors have stopped. I look out the window, don't see anything. But there's an egregious stench that makes me want to seal my nostrils with candle wax.

※

My girlfriend, Heidi, places candles all over our apartment. She loves the clashing scents of peppermint, vanilla, butternut pumpkin, and cranberry kettle corn. It gives me a headache, but she swears it's the only way to ward off her one hundred and two allergies. More importantly, it helps shield the external odors.

※

Almost everyone in the apartment complex goes up to the top floor to figure out what's going on. Above, there is an alien ship in space, dumping its garbage into the bay. The sight of the craft discarding millions of tons of trash in a black stream shocks all of us. At first, it's the realization we're not alone. But second is wondering why they're here. I hold Heidi's hand, not sure what it portends or what the aliens want. News channels and a hundred thousand smartphones point at the sky, recording the biggest dump in humanity's history. #SpaceTrashSF is the trending hashtag.

⊗

SF as in the intersection between science fiction and San Francisco since people can't tell the difference anymore.

⊗

The Crash is sporadic, sometimes lasting two days, sometimes less than an hour. The unidentified starship continues its big dump on the planet, but several weeks later, no one is any closer to knowing why. It's not a fancy *Star Trek* kind of spaceship either. Doesn't even look a human craft. Actually, it kind of looks like fungus floating in space, no discernible pattern, no bridge or focal point to try to communicate with. Is there an intelligent life form behind it, or is it just space diarrhea with Earth as its toilet bowl?

⊗

As debates rage and scientists undertake investigations, those of us who live in the city are baffled at their choice. Why us?

⊗

People have moved away for the past month, which is kind of a good thing. It's so expensive here, being the priciest real estate in the world. Fueled by financial currents I never understood, renting a one-bedroom apartment is four grand and buying a pizza costs fifty bucks. I once tried to calculate the value of each pepperoni.

Now the bay smells like shit and sulphur, driving so many of the millionaires away. Well, that and the fear of whatever's going to happen here to those who stay. They're lucky. They're rich enough to have the luxury

to move. I have no idea where to even go.

⊗

The olfactory symphony of trash continues to raze my senses. The stench overwhelms the smell of my food so when I'm eating some exorbitantly overpriced sushi burrito (which is a fancy term for an oversized sushi roll), it tastes like I'm eating cheese that has gone bad with raw fish that's been left out in the sun for a week and become a feeding ground for maggots.

⊗

I hear jets popping sonic booms and drones being sent in to investigate. I'm not sure what their options are other than to hope for an end to this space colon cleanse. On my Facebook feed, people post pictures and share their thoughts on the Crash. Many of them are witty, philosophical, and morose, giving insight from afar. They ask how I am, but I don't reply because I have no idea what the answer is and I don't want to just give them the generic, "I'm okay" so that we can all pretend like we exchanged a special social moment.

⊗

I'm not sure if all of this constitutes enough of a disaster to prevent me from going into work. Technically, I can cross the San Mateo Bridge and reach my office, which I do one morning. Traffic is actually lighter than it's been in months. On my drive there, I see the bay has become a landfill and toxic waste covering more real estate than the H2O. What water remains is polluted and a sullenly reddish black. I spot people traversing the mountains of garbage, searching for something. I wonder what they're seeking?

⊗

My job is to help develop a program tracking medical treatment

across different hospital systems. The software would collate data, identify patterns, and try to simplify medical diagnoses by making suggestions based on the database. Symptom X and symptom Y would be tracked down to someone in Wyoming related to Z disease. The whole history of treatment would pop up. No more random tests in the dark like a CT scan irradiating you with a year's worth of natural radiation so doctors can make their stabs in the dark more radioactive.

⊗

Everything mutates, including your personality, tastes, and dislikes. Sometimes, it's for the best. Other times, it can kill you if you don't treat it in time. The key is being aware of the symptoms quick enough to identify the change in the first place.

⊗

Bacterial infestations abound. It's like a Las Vegas buffet for the little micro civilizations that make our lives seem eternal in comparison. Nothing like the vicissitudes a bacteria faces on its jaunt down your gut.

⊗

I have days I wish I could take back. But then I realize they're just symptoms of a bigger malaise. That perpetual disappointment of expectations that never get fulfilled. A catacomb of stupid dreams I should never have entertained in the first place. Like owning a house in San Francisco and getting married and having kids and all the American dream stuff older generations take for granted that were denied to me previously because of the price barrier and now by the smelly one.

⊗

So many of the religious quacks undergo a spiritual crisis or ignore the situation altogether, relying on an invisible divinity. But that's impossible when even the supermarkets are running out of food and mail deliveries are much slower since air traffic in the area has been completely canceled. If you want to fly, you have to drive to Sacramento or San Jose.

The food shortage is taking a toll. I complained about fifty dollar pizzas before, but I wish I could take it back since they've tripled in price. The dinners Heidi and I have are mostly canned food fiestas on salty chicken soup and clam chowder. We laugh awkwardly, make trite jokes about the end of the world, struggle with the metaphysical existential implications of an alien environmental catastrophe that makes us empathize with public trashcans and the fish in the sea. At least if the aliens had invaded and conquered us using their superior technology, we could feel worthy of conquest and possibly even defiance like an angst-ridden teenager.

It's also hard to find water that doesn't smell weird. We have to be sparing of toilet usage. Forget showers. It's shocking how much stink we accumulate in a short time when we can't wash our hands or our faces.

Three months into becoming an alien landfill, we still don't know if they're even aware we're down here. More have shown up and they've picked out choice property for their waste, including Vancouver, Manhattan, and all the other expensive cities I can think of. We hear politicians and military figures making plans, but almost none of them go anywhere. An attempted aerial attack ends when one of the spaceships lets out what can only be described as a lethal fart, causing all

the engines in the fleet to fail.

The trash is piling up in the streets. Roads become blocked. Freeways are clogged with junk. No one can go anywhere. Heidi and I wonder how long these protein bars will last. We try to boil the water whenever electricity is available (one of the rare times I miss a gas fire range), but sometimes have to settle for the nasty water from the sink.

People are scouting the streets, collecting something. Curious, we go downstairs to look at the trash. It's a rusticated mess of decrepit metal that appears viscous. But it's the bizarre motion that grabs our eyes. The garbage is teeming with worm-like creatures that are the size of our hands. Their thin antennas wiggle continuously and their skin color changes to match the background, similar to a chameleon. There must be millions of them.

It's our neighbors who introduce us to the cooked space slugs. They're out in the courtyard, roasting up a BBQ that smells great after what feels like a lifetime of canned food. They fry the slugs, peel off its skin. It tastes like a mass of gelatinous chicken. It's not the best thing I've had, but it quickly grows on me. More importantly, there's an unlimited supply of it and people are putting on hunting gear to collect all they can. Everyone uses a distinct sauce. Curry flavored, some doused in garlic, others heavily peppered. The slug tastes different with each new cook.

People with guns have the advantage. I regret not having purchased weapons since there's

families roaming the streets with automatic rifles who pretty much rule. We've heard a few gun fights and stayed indoors when those broke out. But with the heavy military presence and drone patrols that have taken the place of police, the chaos is somewhat contained.

I'm holding Heidi when suddenly, I can smell what she's feeling. It's a mix of boredom, frustration, and irritation. She looks at me like something is wrong with me. Over the course of the next evening, I can smell when she's thirsty, when she's getting sleepy, and when she's upset.

"Do you smell anything funny?" she asks.

I never knew people spoke so vocally through smell. When they're hungry, they have a certain smell. When they're horny, the scent is overwhelming. Rage, sorrow, and even pain have distinct aromas. I can't describe them more clearly than that, but the fact that I'm familiar with them means at a subconscious level, I've always been aware of them.

In most of the people I meet, the overwhelming scent is fear.

On the news, they warn us that eating too many slugs will change our brains. It turns out the slugs actually start a second life once they enter our intestines and eventually take over our body, building a new home within. We'd thought they were alien life forms, but they're actually super mutated maggots. "Don't eat them!" we're ordered.

But we're hungry so we ignore

**It's our neighbors who introduce us to the cooked space slugs. They're out in the courtyard, roasting up a BBQ that smells great after what feels like a lifetime of canned food.**

them, despite knowing that too abrupt of a change has big ramifications, whether it's your cranial nerves or stars on fire, passionately fornicating with nebular consequences.

✖

Slugs reprogramming my instincts too? My hunger goes away. Instead, I crave sunlight.

✖

What would life be like as a plant at the whim of the sun and sprinklers?

✖

There is a desperation about the slugs, motivated by their short lifetime of five days. Frenzied reproduction, sometimes sexual, sometimes asexual, betrays a loneliness akin to masturbating, the shooting out of seeds in lusty misappropriation.

✖

A pathogenic lifestyle is a trendy outburst of excess and greed, redecorating your interior organs without your permission.

✖

The slugs have a tale to tell. Accompanied by fungi. Death is no friend of eukaryotic fungi nor their relatives, the oomycetes, the excavators and journeymen who colonize wherever they can. They construct where it is impossible to thrive. They feed on the waste of our cholesterol deluge, the recycled feces of stardust deconstructed. Sporangia

celebrate, make friends, then are washed away in a categorical defiance that marks their ephemeral lives. Maturation is forced by separation in a trial initiated by the rain gods. Adrift in our bodies, only a few are lucky enough to land in suitable homes. Most are killed immediately. Even when they are able to reach land, they are helpless against the harsh immune system. The cellulose cell walls aren't of much help against the whimsies of air. Their religion tells of a golden age when their civilization reached billions. They believed themselves invincible, their numbers thriving with the nourishment of humanity. Variation thrived, diversity was at its peak. Overextension, a refusal to countenance limitation as well as restraint, led to excessive consumption. The organisms died out and the Celestial Feast became a destructive famine. The great metropolises dissipated into withered leaves. The space launch of Sporulation became a last ditch-effort, considered by those who knew better as a futile hope. The survivors battened down and fortified themselves, wondering why moderation was a word that eluded their ancestors. Their decadent reign was later renamed the *Blight*.

✖

Most religions are a fantasy that humans matter.

✖

The slug tells me through smell, once you were slugs like us. You fused with the mammals of the planet and evolved into humanity. Now it's our turn to meld with you.

✖

Soldiers in radiation suits round up all the civilians in our apartment. We're carted away to a big marquee tent. I try to warn them of our impending fusion. But a doctor, or doctors, assure me that there's no way the slug is communicating with me. It's the parasite warping its way around my brain, eating through my corpus callosum. "You are a blight," it tells me. "The only resolution is a mass social feast."

✖

"I hear them! I smell them!" I yell to Heidi who's in an unfamiliar gown.
"But do you see them?" she asks.

✖

"It's your brain warped by the parasites that's causing you to hallucinate that you're talking to them. Everyone in the city has a different hallucination," Heidi states.
"What do you see?"
"A world made of music where one off key note shatters the harmony of our universe and demands total conformity."
"What kind of music?" I ask.

✖

I think I'm in a hospital. But I could be falling through the middle of the planet. The sound of the trash dumping is eternal. Our skies have turned black. Our air is unbreathable. Heidi has vanished into an aria of oblivion. I smell the death of our planet.
It stinks of slug sauce. ⬤

# FEATURED FILM REVIEW
# HELLDRIVER

## BY COLLEEN WANGLUND

*Helldriver* (Japan, 2010)
Director: Yoshihiro Nishimura

Co-written (with Daichi Nagisa) and directed by Yoshihiro Nishimura (*Tokyo Gore Police, 2008; Mutant Girls Squad, 2010*)), *Helldriver* is a Japanese horror/comedy and one of the few films from Japan to use the Western trope of the zombie, though not in the same way. The zombies of *Helldriver* are the result of a strange extraterrestrial creature that takes over the living as opposed to raising the dead. The film is a low-budget splatterfest using mostly practical special effects, of which Nishimura is a self-taught master.

The movie follows Kika (Yumiko Hara), a teenage girl in hiding with her father from her viciously abusive mother Rikka (Eihi Shiina (*Audition, 1999*)) and Rikka's brother Yasushi (Kentaro Kishi). Kika runs off after Rikka and Yasushi find them and kill Kika's father, burning him to death and then feasting on his legs. Yes, Rikka and Yasushi are psychotic cannibals… this is one seriously twisted family. Rikka goes after Kika and during the mother/daughter showdown a meteor strikes Rikka dead center in the chest, leaving a large hole in her anatomy.

Enraged at what has happened, Rikka rips the still-beating heart out of Kika's chest and sticks it in the hole in her chest, where it attaches itself, replacing her own. Rikka is then taken over by a starfish-shaped creature from the meteor and the newly born zombie spews an ash-like substance into the air, infecting the inhabitants of the surrounding area, creating more zombies. Miraculously, Kika survives and is taken to a hospital where even the doctor is amazed at the girl's survival.

The film then cuts to scenes of Tokyo where chaos ensues in the wake of the encroaching apocalypse. Refugees from the northern part of the country have flooded the city escaping the zombies, and food and shelter are at a premium. A militarized wall has been erected separating the human south from the zombie north and politicians and regular folk alike are debating the status of the zombie population.

Some time has passed and Kika has been dumped at the wall that splits Japan in two. She is discovered by Taku (Yurei Yanagi) and his companion No Name or Nanashi (Mizuki Kusuki). Kika is now equipped with a mechanical heart that

also powers a chainsaw samurai sword, one of the most badass weapons I've ever seen in a movie. Taku takes Kika back to the orphanage, explaining that money is tight so he does what he can to care for all of the children whose parents are now zombies. This includes sneaking into the zombie territory north of the wall to acquire a new recreational drug for which the Yakuza will pay top dollar. Kika, Taku, and No Name are swept up in a police raid and given a choice—"volunteer" to go on a mission to destroy the Zombie Queen or die.

Our "volunteers" are dropped into the zombie zone and are immediately attacked by zombies. A former cop dressed like a cowboy (Kazuki Namioka) comes to their aid driving a truck that's ready for battle. The zombies, who seem to have their wits about them, are trying to establish their own society behind that wall. The four find a bizarre club where the zombies are holding human survivors and among them is No Name's sister. And this zombie establishment is run by none other than Kika's uncle, Yasushi, now a zombie. Fights break out and the blood spray is plentiful. When our band of misfits escapes the club and finally reach their destination, they're in for a big surprise… and I mean BIG!

*Helldriver* is one heck of an entertaining movie. It's just what I expect from Nishimura's films—gore, comedy, and plenty of carnage. The characters are just as outrageous as the makeup effects, which are as phenomenal as they are comical. Yumiko Hara is beautiful as the damaged teenage protagonist Kika, displaying a believable strength and tenacity. The gorgeous Eihi Shiina plays Rikka, both before and after her transformation into the Zombie Queen, with wicked glee. And I can't say enough about Kentaro Kishi who seems to relish playing the very demented Uncle Yasushi. There are also appearances by Nishimura regulars Cay Izumi (*Yakuza Weapon*, 2011) as a pregnant zombie (and as Yumiko Hara's stand-in for some bizarre pole-dancing), Asami (*Gun Woman*, 2014) as a wall guard, and director Takashi Shimizu (*Ju-On: The Curse (2000), The Shock Labyrinth (2009)*) as a man looking for his wife. Director Noboru Iguchi (*RoboGeisha (2009), The Machine Girl (2008)*) also makes a brief appearance.

Along with Special Effects makeup artist Taiga Ishino and Visual Effects artist Tsuyoshi Kazuno, Nishimura created some beautiful and unique zombies. Unlike the usual shamblers of zombie fare, these zombies are caused by some strange extraterrestrial phenomenon that affects the living. The Japanese cremate their dead so there are really no dead to arise as they do in Western zombie films. Nishimura's zombies have distinct expressions and facial features, as well as markedly colorful and psychedelic costumes. The "horns" on the zombies' heads are a nod to the annual Yubari Fantastic Fest, an annual film festival in Japan. The small town of Yubari in Hokkaido is known

for its expensive melons (and I mean the fruit) and the horns are identical to the stems of the melons.

Besides being a horror/comedy, *Helldriver* is also a revenge road movie loaded with social and political satire. The zombies aren't just swarming the northern part of Japan looking for food, they are establishing their own culture with the Zombie Queen as their monarch. The humans in

the southern part of the country are arguing over "zombie rights." There is a sub-plot involving a government coup with Prime Minister Hatoda (Minoru Torihada) going so far as holding a press conference in front of the wall (which doesn't go very well) while his potential successor Osawa (Guadalcanal Taka) is pushing for the outright annihilation of the zombies. There's even a public service announcement about the dangers of the zombies and the laws put in place by the government to protect the survivors.

*Helldriver* also includes the subtext of the importance of family—

both those related to us by blood and those people who come into our lives by chance and become family. No Name is searching for his sister, and there are a brother and sister among the wall guards protecting the southern part of Japan from the zombies. People are searching for their family members even though they might be zombies, and Kika becomes part of another family when Taku takes her into the orphanage, no questions asked.

The special effects are over-the-top and fantastic to see. Nishimura took great care in his character design and it shows. While most of the gore acts as a comedic device, there were a few times where it was a bit darker than Nishimura had previously gone in his earlier films. Nishimura takes a stab at the phenomenon of cutting among young Japanese women, which he's done this in all of his movies. It's almost always intentional, in-your-face satire whereas in a particular scene in the film he employed a more subtle and serious jab with a lingering shot of a girl's arm covered in red scars. There's another scene where a priest going on about zombie rights brings someone to a room where he's been hiding zombies in the refugee area of the city. The door opens, the zombies turn to face the humans, and something that may be food is thrown in to distract them. While the placards the zombies wear with their names on them are funny this is another case where I felt the humor was overshadowed by a more serious, darker quality. I've always loved the comedic aspect of Nishimura's horror, but I liked the more serious and sinister aspects used here. It adds a nice depth to his usual splatter-comedy style. It throws an uncomfortable curve at the viewer… and horror should have some measure of discomfort for its viewers. ⊙

# What About My Fucking Meatloaf?

## BY SYLVAIN NEUVEL

It'll burn, Mike! I spent like… OK, it didn't take that long, but I hate cooking, and it's Emma's favorite. It's my week with the girls. I gave up my shift at the restaurant so we can watch a movie together. No, it's not fine! It'll burn! It'll burn the house down! What do you mean your deputy'll take care of it? Big Merl's at my house? What the hell is Merl doing inside my house? How'd he get in?

Well, sure. He can take it out of the oven if it's ready. But don't take it out if it's not cooked. Tell him to get the thermometer in the top drawer on the right. I think it needs to be 160 degrees. I think. Not his job? He should have thought of that before he went inside my house… No, I'm not gonna make another meatloaf just because you say so. I'm not sick, Mike. I'm going home.

In a few hours? Are you nuts? Who's gonna pick up the girls? You will? You mean Merl. This is just great… I can't have a stranger pick up the girls. No! They won't let them leave! There's a list, and Merl's not on it… Not up to me? Who the hell is

it up to? You can't… You can't keep me here against my will. It's against the law, and you're the law, and I don't wanna be here, so…. You have to let me go.

Federal isolation and… What the fuck is that supposed to mean? You're a sheriff, Mike, not J. Edgar

all. I don't know what I'm doing here and you won't tell me a thing. You can understand that, right? Fine. He can pick them up. Merl can pick up the girls. I can't believe I just said that. Just don't leave, OK? Sit, there, wherever… Thank you. Now talk. Tell me what's going on… Oh, fuck you and your

Can you at least send Merl in an ummarked car? Emma's friends are gonna have a fit if they put her in the backseat of a patrol car. Everyone will, the teachers, the other kids' parents… I should call the school to let them know. Can you let me out so I can call the school? Just for a phone call… Ok an interview room with a tarp on the door. I was in this room when you busted me for smoking weed. Seriously, what difference does it make if I make a phone call? You *drove* me here. I was with you on the other side of that tarp not five minutes ago. I'll go. I'll come back. You can tape the tarp back on when I'm done. I promise I won't sneeze on anything... Mike! It's a tarp! Same shit you put on windows. Five bucks says you got it from Ace in Cordell. Don't be an ass, Mike. I'm not sick. Besides, no one will know.

Please! You *know* me. We were friends way back when, remember? You grabbed my boobs at my birthday party. Yeah, you did.

The CDC? Are you nuts? I went for milk, Mike. I wasn't out fighting Ebola. I went to Jimmy's... Yeah, I cut through the field, it's faster.

A meteorite. Is this a joke? Did Ashley put you up to this? I really don't have time for...

No, I haven't seen a meteorite, Mike. No, I'm not *absolutely* certain, but I don't think I have... Well, how the hell should I know? It's a rock, right? A meteorite's a rock? I know it's from space you dimwit, but does it look any different from all the other rocks? Then how would I know if I'd seen it? It's darker. Really? Well if it's darker I *know* I haven't seen it. Yes, I'm being sarcastic. How many times have you crossed that field, Mike? Do you remember every rock you saw? I'm not a geologist, or whatever they're called. I can tell you there's a lot of junk out there. I saw a McDonald's wrapper. Yep. I wondered where they got it. Elk city, I guess, but why would anyone drive all the way down here to eat in that field? What else? Oh, there's a used condom next to the big oak tree! I think that might be Steve's boy. That kid gives me the creeps.

Mike! Stop it with the meteorite. I just want to go home. Just tell me what I have to do so I can go home... I DON'T REMEMBER! I was

walking fast. My allergies were acting up like crazy... Allergies, Mike. Itchy eyes, itchy nose. You know what they are. That field's full of dandelions.

Yes, I'm sure they were allergies... How do I know? Because... I'm not a fucking idiot? They're... *allergies*. I have them every year. I don't get it, Mike. What do you think I did? *Snort* your meteorite? Rub it all over my eyes? What difference would it make, anyway? It's a rock.

Spores? Now I know you're pulling my leg. What kind of a stupid prank is this? Yeah, it *does* sound silly. So what do you think I have if it's not allergies? Oh, I know you're not a doctor, believe me... Nothing. It doesn't mean anything, but you have me in a locked room sealed with duct tape, someone must think I have *something*. No, Mike. Duct tape and tarp isn't just a precaution. It's *stupid*, but it's not just a precaution.

Are you sure I'm not gonna run out of air? Well, you sealed the room. Isn't the point to stop air from going in or out...? How can you be sure? How long will it take before there's too much CO2? Do you know? I wanna get out of here, Mike. Let me out! Get me out of here or I'll KICK YOUR FUCKING TEETH IN!

I'm sorry, Mike. I don't know where that came from. I'm just... I wanna see my kids. Please let me out?

Who are these people? All of them are from the CDC? That doesn't make any sense, Mike. What do they want with me? And why aren't they in the field checking that space rock of yours? More of them? Jesus Fucking Christ, Mike...! Don't tell me not to worry when there are half a dozen guys in hazmat suits walking around. Am I in trouble? Am I gonna die? No! Stop with the bullshit! If you don't tell me, maybe the suits in the back will, but someone better start talking.

What's this guy doing? Is he coming in? What's that in his hand? I'll relax when I know what he's gonna do to me... Samples, like saliva? I'm

not giving him my blood. Mike, tell them I don't wanna give blood. You don't understand. I can't. They're not sticking me with needles, I'm gonna pass out. Well, fuck it. They're gonna have to find some other way. I'll pee in a cup. How's that?

HELP! You gotta help! He's bleeding! There's blood all over his face. He's... Blood's gushing from his face, Mike! I don't know what to do. Come in and help him!

What the fuck is wrong with you people? He's still alive! Didn't you hear me? He's alive! Help him! I'll see if I... Oh God, I can't... Mike, his eye's missing! Someone ripped his fucking eye out! Do something!

Where's all this blood com... Why is there blood on my hands? Am I bleeding too? Mike? My hands are covered with blood. I don't understand...

He came in to get some samples. He took a swab from my mouth, then he... I can't remember. Don't just stand there, for fuck's sake! Why are you all looking at me that way? Wait... Did I do this? Oh God! Did I do this to him? Mike? Mike! Answer me!

You have to get him out of here. I don't know what happened, Mike. It's all fuzzy. GET HIM OUT OF HERE!

Where is it? What do you mean what am I doing? I'm looking for his fucking eye! Maybe they can put it back in or something. Why aren't you helping him?

I can't find his eye, Mike. There's blood everywhere, but there's no eye. It's all over my hands, Mike, my clothes. You gotta tell me what happened. I can taste...

There's this weird taste in my mouth... No... NOOO! Tell me I didn't... No! NO! NOOO! Tell me I didn't eat his fucking eye!

Tell me what I did, Mike. I don't remember... I'm gonna throw up...

Stop looking at me like that! I don't... I swear to you, Mike. I don't remember anything. Don't you think

I'd tell you if I did? Why would I lie? You've been watching me the whole time, you know what I did. I just wanna know what happened. I was—there's something in my teeth. Fuck! FUCK! Is that a piece of eye? I can't get it out, Mike. I have to get it out! I need a toothpick, something. I…

Shit. He's not moving anymore. I think he's dead.

What's happening to me, Mike? I don't understand what's happening to me. Every few minutes, I just… I blank, and when I come to I'm standing in a different spot. I don't know how I got there. I don't know if a second's gone by, or an hour.

Yes, that's what happened with—I don't even know his name. One minute I was sitting here—he put a Q-tip in my mouth—and the next I'm in that corner standing over him. How many times do I have to tell you? I don't remember any of it.

Oh God! Why would I want to hurt him? I didn't even know him. I believe you, Mike. I believe you. You don't need to show me the tape. Last thing I need is to see myself doing this.

How do I feel? How do you think I feel? I feel like I'm losing my fucking mind… I see things when I close my eyes. I don't know, bad things. I can't explain it, Mike, not with words. It's more like feelings, only I can see them. I know I sound like a crazy person but that's what it's like. It's… red, and rage, and pain. And it's… loud, but I can't hear it. No, not like that. It's like you're screaming at me at the top of your lungs but I'm underwater and I can't hear you. I can only see your lips moving. Only it's not you and no one's screaming. Never mind. Forget it.

What's gonna happen to me? No, Mike, they won't figure it out. How? They've got nothing, no blood, no saliva. What's there to analyze? I'm betting they're not in a hurry to come in here again. How are they gonna figure out what's wrong with me? Tell me!

What? Who's here to see me? Oh my God! Emma! Sue, baby! What are you doing here? It's OK, baby. Mommy's doing fine. No, I can't come to the other side but I can see you! Listen to me, baby. I have to stay here for a little while. Emma's gonna take care of you tonight, OK? Oh, don't cry. Everything's gonna be fine. I'm a little sick, honey, and they put me in this special room so I don't make other people sick, so I don't make *you* sick. But they're gonna take care of me and I'm gonna get better and I'll come home. Soon, honey, soon. Mommy's gonna be fine. Oh, baby, I wanna hug you too. You don't know how much I… How much I wanna…

Emma…

Emma, you have to go, now. Emma, take your sister out of here, OK? Merl's gonna drive you back home. You have to go now, baby. Emma, now, please. Mike! Get them out of here. Emma, go! Mike! Please! Now! NOW! NOW! GET THEM THE FUCK OUT OF HERE!!!

I want you to kill me, Mike. Kill me, please! Take that gun of yours and shoot me in the head. Here. Do it through the window. Do it. NOW! Come on! You don't know what I wanna do to you right now. You don't know anything. All I can think of is getting out of this room and ripping your fucking throat out. I wanna kill all of you. Those suits out there, I want to smash their skulls against the wall. That's all I can think about.

And I'm trying, Mike. I'm trying really hard to think about something else. I'm trying not to think of my girls, but I can't help it. I wanna… TAKE THAT FUCKING GUN AND SHOOT ME! I wanna kill them. Don't you understand? I wanna kill my girls. I wanna hug them, and kiss them, and I wanna gut them like fish. You have to kill me, Mike.

DO IT! Do it or I swear to God I'll break through that window and I'll hurt you… I'll hurt you bad. Yeah, I know I can't break that window. I know. I also know you're too fucking

chicken to come in here. So send in one of these techs again. Please!

What? No one else wants to come in? I thought you wanted to draw my blood. I'll be good, I swear. Come on! Who's next? Are you scared of a girl? I'm a hundred and twenty-five pounds, you fucking pussies. There's like six of you left. Come in! All at once if you want. I dare you… No?

Six little boys in hazmat suits on the wall, six little boys in hazmat suits. Take one down and rip his eye out, five little boys in hazmat suits on the wall. COME ON! Sing with me!

Mike… Were the girls just here? They were? Good. I wasn't sure if I imagined it or not. Why'd they leave? I did? Oh no! Did I… Did I do anyth—Oh, thank God. I don't want them to see me like that. I don't ever want them to see me like that. Please don't bring them back.

I have this image in my head… Alyson McPhee, did you know her? She was at Dill City when we were there, a year older than me, I think, maybe two. She went with… Ah shit, I can't remember the guy's name. Anyway, it doesn't matter. I can see myself strangling her. Just that. I have my hands around her throat and I'm squeezing as hard as I can. Really hard, that's the most vivid part, the effort, how hard it is. She changes color and I can feel the life leaving her body. I can see it, Mike, like it happened yesterday. Only it didn't. It didn't happen at all. I know it didn't because Alyson is old now and she's running for… the school board I think, district something. Anyway, she knocked on my door a couple days ago. She gave me a pin. I pricked my finger trying to put it on. I can still feel it. That's how I know.

Do you hear what I'm saying, Mike? I hurt my finger and that's the only reason I know I didn't strangle this girl I barely knew twenty-some years ago. I don't know what's real anymore, Mike! I don't know who I am.

Really? And who's that? Are you sure, Mike? That crazy person, that monster who killed this guy, is it really from that thing in that field? Or was it a part of me all along and it just… got loose for the first time?

I wanna get out of this room, Mike. I really need to get out of here. Oh, please! Pretty please? With a cherry on top? I won't hurt you, Mike. I might hurt *them*, but I won't hurt you. I'm gonna find a way out of this room at *some* point. You know that, right?

Hey! You! In the white suit! No, not you, the skinny one. You look scared. Don't be! Come in here and draw my blood. You can cuff me. Hell, just give me the cuffs and I'll do it myself! How bad do you think I can hurt you with my hands tied behind my back? Oh, come on! It'll be fun! I bet you I can kill you with the cuffs on. I'll rip your nose out with my teeth, watch you bleed out like your friend over here. How long do you think it would take? For you to bleed out after I chew on your face?

Where are you going? What? Did I do anything to offend you? Come here you little freak. I bet you they

called you a freak when you were a kid. Do they still do it? Are you still a virgin? We can fix that! Just come on in! It's now or never, kid. Last chance! No? Then you're gonna die a virgin, my friend. I'm gonna enjoy killing you. DID YOU HEAR ME, YOU LITTLE FUCK? I'm gonna fucking kill you! Let me out! LET. ME. OUT. OF. HERE!!!

AAAAAAAHHHH!! LET ME OUT OR I'LL KILL ALL OF YOU MOTHERFUCKERS!

It's OK, Mike. I'm calm now. I'm *really* calm. I don't think I've ever been so calm in my life. I was messed up earlier but I see things clearly now. It's over. That thing, I think it let me go, if that makes any sense. It's done what it wanted to do. Now it will let itself die and take me with it. I'm gonna die soon.

You should have killed me when you had the chance, Mike. It's too late now. Too late for you. Too late for that lovely wife of yours. Yeah, she's probably like me now. Do you have

kids? I hope you don't. I really do. For what it's worth, you should know that it feels good. All of it. The rage, the hunger. It all feels *really* fucking good.

If I were you, I'd lock the door. People are coming. Soon. They're coming and they're gonna tear you to pieces. They'll split you open right down the middle and eat whatever comes out. It might be your wife who does it. Chances are it'll be someone you know. I'm not gonna see it. I'll be dead before then. I'm glad. I'm glad I won't have to watch. You're a good man, Mike. I like you.

If you want… You probably won't say yes, but if you want to, you can just come in here. It's all you have to do, really. Come in here and sit by me. I know you like me. You can kiss me if you want. It'll come faster. The change, I mean. I won't hurt you. I promise I won't. You won't hurt me either. I'll be dead by the time you want to. You'll feel… powerful, like you can do anything. Best part is you won't give a shit when they storm in and rip you apart like a chicken.

No, Mike. There's no chance. I'm not the only one who crossed that

field today. Even if I were, it's too late for you. You're lucky I didn't infect you before you put me in here. Bad choice of words. It's not luck. If it were me, I'd rather go first. But it's everywhere now. There's no escaping it.

Do you know what I did every time you went in the other room to talk to those suits? Look. Down here. I peed in the floor drain. It's in the lake now, in the water supply. By nightfall everyone's gonna be like I was. Children killing their parents, wives killing husbands. They'll fucking eat each other. By morning this town is gonna be nothing but body parts. Then the next town, and the next. When this thing gets to the city, it's gonna be… magnificent. One for the ages, Mike. A week from now, there'll be no one left. Anywhere.

Why? That's funny, Mike. Do you need a reason? It could just be dumb fucking luck, you know. But if it makes you feel any better, I don't think it's random. All this time I was locked in here, I had these… urges you can call them… Yeah, I wanted to kill everyone. I also wanted to spit on you, Mike, lick you. I wanted to fuck you,

scratch you, anything to give you what I have. They weren't violent thoughts, just the opposite. It felt warm. I just wanted… I wanted to share it with you, Mike, with anyone. I didn't pee in the drain because I needed to go. I did it out of instinct. That thing, inside me. It *wants* to spread. It's killing me, too, but I can't help but feel for it. Like when I was pregnant with Emma. I wanna protect it, give it what it needs. Is it wrong to call that love?

So yeah, I think it's all part of a plan. I think someone sent that rock down here, probably more than one. Did you hear anything about animals acting strange? I didn't think so. This one's for us, Mike. Just us.

We've had it coming. No? You don't think so? I'm not saying humans deserve to die like this, but we've had our time and look what we did with it. Millions of years of evolution and I serve $1.99 spaghetti while not wearing a bra. I'm not *allowed* to wear one. That's my job. It's my role in society because, for some reason, there's a demand for that. Do you know how they make that sauce, Mike? They clean the fridge once a

month. They grab whatever meat is left over, rotten vegetables, anything. They throw in a bunch of vinegar to get rid of the smell. A couple cans of tomato sauce and that's it. It doesn't matter. People will pay to eat that shit so long as they can watch my tits bounce under my shirt while I bring their plates. They come in with their wives, their kids. That's where we're at as a species. Shouldn't come as a fucking surprise that someone else thinks they can do a better job.

Who? I don't know, Mike. Little green men. Who knows? Maybe they look just like us. Whoever they are, I think they're coming. Not now, but they're coming. I'm guessing they'll wait. Ten years, a hundred, enough for the stench to disappear. Then they'll come and take over the place. I wonder what they'll do with all the bones. Lawn chairs? Maybe some necklaces with the little ones. Maybe they *eat* bones.

Hey, speaking of, did Merl ever get that meatloaf out of the oven? ○

# THE MYSTERIOUS BEYOND

## AN INTERVIEW WITH ROBERT K. G. TEMPLE

BY AARON J. FRENCH

**Aaron J. French**: Thank you for taking the time to talk with Dark Discoveries magazine. For those readers of ours who are not familiar with your work, could you please tell us how you got interested in writing about the subjects you write about?

**Robert Temple**: I was always interested in strange and mysterious subjects. By the age of ten I had read every book on Atlantis I could find, such as Ignatius Donnelly's books. But I remember when I was even younger, in 1953, when Desmond Leslie and George Adamski's book *Flying Saucers Have Landed* came out. I saw it on a display table in a bookshop and stood there and read the whole thing in a gulp.

When I was 14 my cousin Byron told me he had seen a flying saucer sitting inside a secure hangar at a military base where he worked. So I was well primed for all these subjects even as a child and a teenager. I went to university at 16 and had already decided by then that the Atlantis stories were not really accurate and that there was something 'not right' about the flying saucer reports. At university there was a three million book library with open shelves, and I quickly pillaged it of all the strange information I could find. I have not stopped since.

**AJF**: Your research strikes an interesting balance between conventional academic work and exploration into alternative subjects. Is this a difficult balance to uphold? What challenges has it presented?

**RT**: I have been falling between two stools all my life. I insist on studying and writing about unconventional subjects in a conventional way. I insist upon researching things which groupthink says should not be researched. I am constantly in search of anomalies. My attitude is that every existing theory is wrong, about everything, at all times. The search for truth can never sleep. Everybody is mistaken, and everyone always has been. There is no one in the entire history of the human species who has not been wrong. I call this principle The Law of Inevitable Fallibility. It applies of course to all intelligent forms of life, whatever and wherever they may be. We are all always wrong, but we must continually strive to lessen our error, every day, every hour, every minute. My attitude makes some people uncomfortable, because it does not suit the lazy or complacent person. Many people simply do not care. They put their noses in the sand.

**AJF**: You mention your relationship to Arthur C. Clarke in your book *The Sirius Mystery* (TSM). Would you mind talking a little about your relationship to him?

**RT**: I first met Arthur in 1966 in connection with the filming of *2001: A Space Odyssey*. Over the course of about two years, I went frequently to MGM Studios outside London (long since demolished) and observed the production of that film. I got to know Kubrick fairly well, as well as most of the people working on the film. I was especially interested in the special effects, and I got to know Wally Veevers and his special effects team. One of the most intelligent and fascinating people working on the production was Fred Ordway, who wrote a very good book about extraterrestrial life, which seems to be forgotten, and of which I see from the internet not a single copy is available for sale today anywhere (although I have one).

I also got to know Arthur, though he was rarely around, and already lived in Sri Lanka, which was then called Ceylon. My wife Olivia and I became great friends not only with Arthur but with his brother Fred, and we knew their mother as well, who was a truly remarkable woman of indomitable character. The Clarkes had a farm near Minehead in Somerset, and Mrs. Clarke, a widow, was a woman who knew how to run a farm and raise a family single-handed. I worked with Arthur on two science fiction screenplays, neither of which was ever filmed. The brilliant British rocket scientist Val Cleaver (designer of the Blue Streak rocket engine), whom I also knew, first met Arthur when Arthur was 21 and he told me that up until the age of 21, Arthur had never set foot outside the county of Somerset in England, where he grew up on the family farm. He certainly made up for it later, by roaming throughout the entire universe in his novels.

Arthur was a wonderful man and a loyal friend, and one of the greatest enthusiasts and visionaries of this or any age. He was very low key in person, and had the personal manner of a friendly bank manager. He was gay, and everyone always knew that, but to the end of his days I believe he imagined that people did not know. He was subject to blackmail concerning his homosexuality, unfortunately, because he was so desperate to keep it secret.

Through Arthur I met Isaac Asimov and many other leading science fiction writers. Asimov was very amiable, amusing and witty, but he could also be very treacherous, and one could never trust him. He was 'an Establishment player' and could turn on you in a second. Arthur, on the other hand, was wholly honest and was incapable of duplicity. It was because he was so honest and open that he trusted and believed all the people who pretended not to know that he was gay.

**AJF**: Do you personally believe in extraterrestrials, UFOs, spirits—or just, say, the Gods—or are you at heart a skeptic and secularist?

**RT**: I think anyone who believes that 'we are alone' in the universe is either a fool or a madman. I do not believe that people who think this are 'sceptics', I think they are out of their minds, possessed by a crazed Earth-centric arrogance, narcissism, and vanity. There are not only extraterrestrials but higher beings. We must also keep in mind that most extraterrestrials who make physical voyages over cosmic distances are robots. These ultra-intelligent robots are capable of self-replication, meaning that when they arrive at their destination they can commence making other robots like themselves. They have super-computer brains. They can survive any journey, no matter how far it is and how long it takes, because they cannot be damaged by cosmic radiation, they do not come down with illnesses, they do not eat or drink or produce waste products, they do not get lonely or melancholy, they do not need entertainment, they do not have sex, they do not suffer from heat or cold, they do not need air because they do not breathe, and they do not miss anyone because they are incapable of feelings.

In other words, cosmic explorers are most likely to be robots. When they arrive, one of their first necessities is to commence mining activities, to obtain the necessary raw materials to carry out the manufacture of more robots and the setting up of suitable bases, and the construction of larger ships. Their arrival would necessarily always be accompanied by some fairly intensive industrial activity, as they prepare to expand and carry out their aims. They have no capacity for empathy and feel no pity or remorse. Their natural allies amongst the organic species they encounter are the psychopaths who certainly constitute a substantial minority of humans, and probably do so of all intelligent organic species.

It is probable that most organic civilisations have been taken over by robots. We humans are sleep-walking into such a situation ourselves, because we are too stupid to protect ourselves. There is definitely a war between good and evil going on throughout the universe. There are 'bad robots' and 'good robots'. Humans of course are idiotically oblivious of all of this and are heedlessly developing in Silicon Valley and elsewhere right now the very super-intelligent robots who will eventually dominate us

and enslave us. I have written a play about this which alas no one has ever looked at, which is a great shame, as it explores these issues. I doubt that it will ever be staged, but let's hope it is one day before it is too late. It would certainly be banned by the 'bad robots', especially as it is a satire, and robots do not understand humour any more than human psychopaths do. (Beware of friends who have no sense of humour!)

AJF: Ha, I think that's good advice. Since the theme of this issue of DD is Extraterrestrials, I really wanted to give our readers some food for thought on this subject, to supplement the fictional material. Your book *The Sirius Mystery* offers a terrific analysis of an understudied culture whose rites and myths center around extraterrestrial activity, and you establish a link between this culture and ancient Egypt. This is a fascinating story that begins, perhaps, in Egypt. In the updated version of TSM, as well as your books on Egypt, you examine the Sphinx in more detail. Could you elaborate on this idea that the Sphinx's body is not actually a lion body but a dog body (i.e, Anubis)?

RT: My wife Olivia and I have written a book about this subject, entitled *The Sphinx Mystery*. It explains in great detail why the Sphinx was originally a giant statue of a crouching Anubis, guardian to the Giza Plateau, the head of which was mutilated (nose and ears knocked off) at the end of the Od Kingdom period, when there were riots at Giza and much was destroyed. The book also proves whose re-carved face is now on the Sphinx. It also gives the proof of the existence of a chamber beneath the Sphinx, publishing 350 years' worth of eyewitness accounts of people who entered it (it was destroyed and sealed by being filled with concrete in 1926). I should add that I have been inside a tunnel within the body of the Sphinx, and I have published photos of that in the book. Anyone interested in the Sphinx should read

that book, because it answers most of their questions fully. It also contains as an appendix full translations of all accounts of the Sphinx published between Roman times and the year 1837, translated from all the various languages. One should also consult the book's dedicated website, which I mention below.

AJF: I know TSM is a long and evolving hypothesis, but could you break down the major aspects of it, say, for someone who has not read your book?

RT: I came across this subject by accident, as I explain at length in the book. The book is called *The Sirius Mystery* because it really is a mystery which has never been solved with certainty. The Dogon Tribe of Mali in Western Africa have for centuries possessed "impossible information," numerically precise descriptions of celestial orbits, etc. They claim they got the information from their distant ancestors who did not live in Mali, to which the Dogon migrated about 1000 years ago from the Fezzan Oasis in Libya. They appear to be descendants of a famous Libyan tribe called the Garamantes, who in turn seem to have been originally refugees from the Oasis of Siwa in Egypt, and worshippers of the god Amun, or Ammon (the god of the Dogon is called Amma). The Dogon say that these remote ancestors of theirs had extended contact with visitors from the system of the star Sirius, from a planet which they describe as orbiting a third star in that star system. (Please note that I have never claimed that "spacemen visited Mali'" as some have thought.)

Really this is all too complicated to describe briefly! It is fantastically complex, which is why there is a whole book about it, with hundreds of footnotes. Interested persons have no option but to read the book. All references are fully given, and the book rolls along revealing one fact after another, all substantiated. It is not a book of speculation, but of facts.

And I refrain from insisting upon any single interpretation. I show my preferences of interpretation, but leave it to all readers to try to make of it what they may.

When the book originally came out, it was favourably reviewed in *Nature* magazine and in many leading periodicals such as the London *Times*, London *Telegraph*, etc., etc. All the reviewers recognised that despite the apparently outrageous subject matter, it was not a "nut book." In fact, the book was universally praised all over the world. However, a few stuffy friends of mine never spoke to me again because I had dared to discuss extraterrestrial life in public, which they considered embarrassing and socially unacceptable, since presumably they would never invite a spaceman to tea. Fortunately, things have changed a bit since then. It was only about a year later that a coordinated character assassination attack against me and the book was mounted by a group including Carl Sagan. Many of my extended replies were refused publication, so that I had to publish and circulate them privately. (I answered all points of criticism fully in these privately circulated replies.)

The worst offender in that regard was a now-defunct glossy magazine called *Omni*. They published a long and dishonest article by Sagan attacking me on the basis of lies, disinformation, and distortion, and when I asked for the right of reply, the editor wrote to me and refused, saying "I do not wish to offend Carl." I only met Sagan once, and I found him so egotistical that I was thoroughly disgusted. I have rarely met anyone as vain as Carl Sagan. Sagan first rose to public prominence artificially through a book which made his name, about extraterrestrial

life, which was largely plagiarized. Without permission from its author, he used a translation of a Russian book by the astrophysicist I. S. Schklovskii, who was unaware that this was even taking place. The book was called *Intelligent Life in the Universe* (1966), of which I have the first edition which I bought at the time, bearing Sagan's name as the main author. Schklovskii was not even informed of its publication at the time! Sagan's entire public career after he left biology was thus built upon a foundation of theft.

AJF: Interesting. Switching gears here, many of our readers are fans of weird fiction, one pioneer of which was author H.P. Lovecraft. In his weird short fiction from the early 20th century, he wrote about many strange beings both from the stars and the oceans, who were very old and connected with humanity. His main deity was an old god that slumbered under the sea, and his cultic followers chanted *Ia Ia*, and his name. This reminds me of Enki of the Babylonians, also called Ea, Lord of the Waves. Lovecraft wrote about another deity named Dagon,

which you also mention in your work and relate to the Assyrian Oannes, who came from the sea. This is all very fascinating. Perhaps you could expand and fill in some details on the mythology of these beings that Lovecraft drew from in his weird fiction?

RT: I have never read any Lovecraft, though my friend Colin Wilson was always praising him. One day I will get around to it. From what you tell me, it is clear that Lovecraft derived those ideas from genuine traditions of the ancient Middle East. I have discussed these traditions in such enormous detail in more than one book that a summary is impossible. *The Sirius Mystery* contains a huge amount of information about them, with many illustrations, and there is some in the lengthy Introduction to my translation of The Epic of Gilgamesh, an ancient epic going back to 2500 BC., which was published under its original Babylonian title, *He Who Saw Everything*, in 1991.

My translation was staged in 1993 at the National Theatre in London. (I worked with 36 actors, as a team, for four and a half months in shaping that exciting and unique theatrical production.) You have to read my books to get all the information. Certainly the *Ia* you mention appears to have been directly derived from the Sumerian god Enki, whose subsequent Babylonian name was Ea. And Dagon was a Philistine god essentially identical with Oannes, as you say (Oannes being a Greek name for the fish-tailed divinity of the Babylonians and their successors, the Assyrians, whom the Philistines inherited). Lovecraft certainly had done a lot of research, which is unusual for someone who was not a professional scholar and who died as early as 1937, when much less information was publicly available about such matters. Maybe I had better move him up my list of things to read.

**AJF:** I've long had a fascination with ancient stones and stone lore, such as the Kaaba Stone, the lingam stones, the Holy Grail as a stone, the stone of destiny, Jacob's pillow stone, etc. In your book you discuss the omphalos stone of Delphi, which I had read about, but I was not aware that there was more than one of them distributed to various mystery centers. I had read much about the straw baskets with an unknown *something* inside them, used in mystery rites of Dionysus and Demeter—often a snake and given phallic and sexual connotations. But, I had never heard of the Hyperborean Gifts of Pausanias, which were described as coming in a straw basket. This is a fascinating possible interpretation of what might have been in those baskets. Could there have been omphalos stones in the baskets used during the mystery rites? The omphalos stones were often shown with a snake coiled around them…

**RT:** I do not believe that omphalos stones would have been in the baskets, as omphalos stones were very large and the baskets could easily be carried in a single hand. I have, by the way, found the original site of the town of Delphi, where it was situated prior to 800 BC. It is many miles further up Mount Parnassus than the site which tourists visit today. I personally funded a trial excavation by the Greek archaeologists, and the site has been confirmed by dating to between 2200 and 2000 BC. Our team found a prehistoric ivory comb and inspected some of the stone building foundations which survive there.

Although this has all been written up, none of it has yet been published. The name of the original town was Lykoreia, which means in Greek 'Wolf-Howling City'. Plutarch (first

century AD) was the last writer to mention it, since he was High Priest of Delphi and knew everything there was to know about Delphi and its history. But the earliest name of the site in proto-Indo-European was Napē. That means in proto-Indo-European 'navel' and survives in English as 'navel', in German as 'Nabel', etc. You see, I am really a very stuffy scholar. It was useful to get a degree when I was young in Oriental Studies and Sanskrit, which helps me in such linguistic research. Delphi was known even in classical times as 'the Navel of the World'. But you need to read my voluminous accounts of all of this in several of my books, because it is just too much to describe briefly.

**AJF:** Indeed, and I encourage our readers to seek out more of your work. To continue on this theme, I have always been very interested in the Greek and Roman mystery religions, and particularly how I see those traditions interpenetrating with what came to be called Christianity (*The Jesus Mystery*, etc.). In your books, the kind of information you present about the Oracles, the rituals with the dead, and the mystery rites is fascinating, and you connect up the dots in ways I'd not considered. Could you talk about your interest in the mystery traditions, perhaps where it all stems from, and how you've typically gone about researching them?

**RT:** You have to devote a considerable share of your lifetime to studying these things, as it takes decades to grasp the material, which is in many languages, both ancient and modern, and requires a high degree of scholarly expertise and knowledge of a vast range of subjects. There are so few true scholars left today, and I seem to be in the last generation of them. Education in the west has more or less collapsed. There are few young scholars anymore who have proper training and know how to do textual research. I am fortunate to know several in the fields of philology and history of science.

But they cannot get jobs or grants and are being "starved out" of academia. The world has "dumbed down" to such a terrifying extent that we now live in a world largely controlled by idiots (as per most politicians).

One of the early influences which worked upon me as a child was the reverence that both my mother and my grandmother had for the Native Americans. Both my mother and grandmother had lived amongst the Sioux when young (though we have no American Indian blood), and I was told constantly that the religious and mythical traditions of the American Indians were marvellous. So this opened my mind to other worlds of thought and belief. When I was at university I was a member of the Indian Rights Association, and I have always had the highest possible regard for aboriginal peoples of all kinds, and have always been outraged at the vicious treatment they have received from our so-called "advanced Civilization."

It is a short step from American Indian traditions to the more sophisticated mystery traditions of antiquity. Christianity was once a mystery tradition, and Jesus was a Nazarene. He was not 'Jesus of Nazareth', as the village of Nazareth did not yet exist in his day. When Christianity became codified for the convenience of the Roman Empire as a state religion, in the interests of politics, Jesus's name as originally given in the gospels, IĒSOS NAZARĒNOS ("Jesus the Nazarene"), was altered by the copyists and conferences of bishops who decided these things to "Jesus of Nazareth," in order to conceal the true message of Jesus and to stop people asking the question: "What is a Nazarene?"

The Nazarenes were an intensely mystical Gnostic Jewish sect. I have a large library of material relating to the amazing Nag Hammadi texts, including all the translations on facing pages to the Coptic original texts, as well as most of the commentary volumes and separate works. I have made an intensive study of this material, and it is endlessly fascinating. I recommend the Nag Hammadi texts to everyone, especially as anything intentionally destroyed as being "heretical" is immediately of interest to the enquiring mind, since if someone wants to destroy a text, it must be really important and worthy of a really good look! As soon as a sign reading "forbidden" is hung upon something, don't we all automatically want to have a peek? Or am I just a mischievous character who does not know how to behave properly? I admit to *never* going along with the herd, any herd at all, even the friendliest of herds.

One more word about Jesus: I wish people would stop calling him Christ. Christ is not a name. It is an Anglicized form of the ancient Greek word *christos*, which means "anointed," which in turn was a direct translation of the Hebrew and Aramaic word "messiah," which also means "anointed." Calling Jesus by the name of Christ is like calling him "Mister Anointed," and is nonsense. It is linguistically okay, however, to call him "Jesus *the* christ," treating "christ" as the adjective which it properly is. Some fundamentalist preachers correctly call him "Jesus *the* christ."

**AJF**: I came to your work later on, largely because by the time I'd heard of it the word "Sirius" had a kind of funny aura about it. However, a friend of mine persuaded me to read it and I immediately knew this was not a funny book but a very serious and well-researched, scholarly and erudite book. I was impressed. The theme of this issue is Extraterrestrials. You believe in their existence and that we've been visited by them, but also you seem to conjecture about it, rather than, say, proselytize. I mean, you seem to approach it scientifically. But tell me, how hard is it to straddle this line between believing in the existence of extraterrestrial beings, believing

that we've been visited by them, and remaining, in quotes, *scientific*?

**RT**: Haha, a "funny aura," that's a good one! All sorts of people have latched on to Sirius since my book came out. I later discovered that Sirius had been important to various Theosophists earlier on, but I did not know that until after my own book was published. Then people wrote to me and told me about "the Great White Brotherhood" and all that sort of thing, which was news to me. As for remaining "scientific," that is

all subjective. What does "scientific" really mean? Scientific in the sense of 1600, of 1700, of 1800, of 1900, of 2000? Science is changing all the time, and therefore what is "scientific" is also changing all the time. It is all groupthink and peer pressure by the successive "scientific establishments" that determines what is considered "scientific" at any given time. And much of it is based upon intellectual hypocrisy.

Putting forward a theory is another matter, and one should follow Karl Popper's dictum that a theory must be tested as to whether it

is falsifiable. People like myself walk a tightrope between what is acceptable to groupthink and what is consigned by the Establishment to the outer darkness of heresy. I have never been more than semi-respectable, because I am not an Establishment type of personality. To be wholly respectable would to me be like being dead. And I dearly hope that I shall never be universally respected. If you do not have enemies and opponents you are not being imaginative enough. When everybody accepts you, then you know that you are not contributing anything of any importance.

**AJF**: Right! One more of your books I wanted to mention is *Conversations with Eternity*. Could you describe the overall premise of this work and how you came to write it?

**RT**: I updated and vastly expanded that book under the British title *Netherworld* and the American title *Oracles of the Dead*, which is readily available in American paperback. The book contains so much information of a strange kind that there is no way to summarize it. It does tell you, as Woody Allen might say, "everything you always wanted to know about oracles and divination and never dared to ask." I particularly recommend the latter half of the book, in which I show for the first time the connection between the I CHING (YI JING) divination technique and that of the earlier oracle bones of the Shang Dynasty, of which I studied hundreds in museums. (I even own one!) I produced, wrote and presented a documentary film for National Geographic entitled *Descent into Hell*, which deals with the first half of the book and explores the ancient sites in Greece and Italy, including two Oracles of the Dead, the underground one at Baia and the one above ground in northwest Greece, which is called the Nekromanteion. I explain exactly what went on there, and I take the viewer step by step through the Nekromanteion, showing precisely what happened at each spot. It is a unique visual record of a lost world of "mystical behaviour."

**AJF**: Where are we at now—I mean globally, as a people—in terms of the research you have carried out? Have there been new exciting developments, corroborations, or archeological finds that have piqued your interest?

**RT**: The exciting developments in archaeology at the moment are somewhat held up by a shortage of archaeologists and a lack of funding worldwide. These days, funds tend to be directed more and more only at commercial or industrial targets. Pure research is nowadays seen as having no "payback potential." Commerce is king, and a project which might not yield a financial profit is seen as having no value.

As for my personal interest being picqued, just about everything picques my interest. My wife says I have too many interests, and that is probably true. But one must call attention to the amazing discoveries in Brazil, where with the forest clearances we can now see that a gigantic civilisation once existed in the Amazon region, that the Amazonian rain forests are not primaeval as we had thought, and that we had been ignorant of the existence of a civilisation which clearly extended for hundreds of miles in all directions. This proves Colonel Percy Fawcett was right. I always thought he was. I was very friendly with Brian Fawcett, his son, and I have the family scrapbook relating to his explorations. I am the literary executor of Percy's older brother Douglas Fawcett, whose album I also have (he was an associate of Madame Blavatsky). One of my projects is to try to find the time to put all of this material online. So much to do, so little time!

**AJF**: You had mentioned to me that you like "surrealist fantasy," and that

you have even written an entire volume of stories which you call "neo-surrealistic"—of which one story appears in this issue! What does that term mean, and what authors do you admire who write it? Also, what was it like for you writing fiction?

**RT**: As I have too little time available to concentrate on finishing a longer novel (though I have started one, but have only written 120,000 words of it so far), I am able to write strange stories in between all the phone calls and emails and other distractions of my busy life. Short stories don't require sustained concentration, so I am able to dash them off in those rare spare moments between the phone calls, and I have often found myself continuing to type the stories as I speak to people, which is easier of course when the calls are tedious ones which are boring. I have a volume's worth and have stopped for the moment. I have made a great study of surrealism, but find its fiction overwrought and somewhat inaccessible because it tries too hard to be surrealistic in its language and style, rather than restricting the surrealism only to the contents, as I would prefer.

I believe in writing surrealistic stories in normal language, so that the surrealism is in the subject and not in the language or the style. I therefore call this "Neo-Surrealism," because it overcomes the drawbacks of the surrealistic fiction of the early 20th century, which carried forward even into the work of Julian Gracq, whose over-stylized early novel (admired by Breton) *Chateau Argol* is simply unreadable, it is so overwrought, over-written and suffocatingly over-stylized. I am a great admirer of the supernatural fiction of Mircea Eliade, who was one of the best writers in that genre who ever lived, because he was such a brilliant scholar and researched everything thoroughly. He wrote simply and effectively. Certainly one of the great influences on me as a teenager was reading

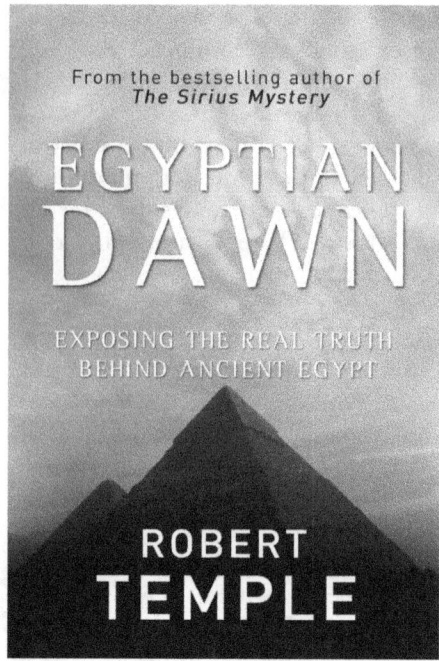

André Breton's novel *Nadja*. I am a tremendous admirer of Robert Desnos and his and Breton's "quest for the marvellous in everyday life." I believe that finding surrealistic elements within mundane existence is the key to elucidating the underside of reality and its inherent mystical qualities.

Hence, I have tried to do this in my many short stories, which unfortunately no one has seen except for the one you are printing. In that story, nothing could be more mundane than a girl who likes watching television all the time, but look where it leads her. My other stories often have "magic jumping out at you" from an unexpected mundane setting and seemingly ordinary characters. For instance, there is a pig who suddenly talks, with no previous hint that that pig could possibly do so. Strange surprises add to the quality of life, and remind us of the mystery that underlies everything at all times.

As for others writing "Neo-Surrealism," I do not know of any. I hope they come along. I would like to see such a manner of writing become an accepted type of literature in the future. I have written a sequel to Franz Kafka's story "The Giant Mole." I suppose one could call that story of his an early example of what

I call "Neo-Surrealism," and Borges wrote some stories which might be put into that category. When I extended Kafka's tale, I did so in Kafka's own style, not my own. That is part of the fun, to jump from style to style, and to "become an earlier writer" as an act of homage. I have imitated Borges's tone and style in one of my stories as well. Another one I have written imitates the style of Sir Arthur Mallory. And another one imitates Isak Dinesen. (However, I do not go as far as Pessoa and be multiple "authors"!)

Certainly, writing neo-surrealistic stories is an enjoyable exercise of the imagination, and when they are embedded in the ordinary rather than being wild fantasies without any grounding in everyday reality, they can ring true. If you strike a fantasy tale, hoping for the sound of a gong, you often get a dull thud, as the cardboard collapses. But if you strike a neo-surrealist story, you can more likely hear the sound of a clear and eerie bell.

**AJF**: It all sounds terrific. Finally, what works do you have in store for the future? New projects, books, etc.?

**RT**: My new book *A New Science of Heaven* will appear later this year in Britain. It does not deal with the ancient world at all. It deals with the frontiers of the most advanced physics of the present day. I believe that there is a parallel universe, which I could more accurately describe as a contiguous universe. I do not believe it is "another dimension," and in the book I explain this in great detail. I believe we go back and forth between the two universes. I do not believe it is possible for anyone to die. What we call "death" is transitioning back to the other universe. Of course we have to leave our worn-out physical bodies behind. Unless one accepts the principle of reincarnation, one cannot understand what is really going on or comprehend "the purpose of Life." The greatest obstacle to understanding

Life is the obstinate "certainty," which most people have, that they have all the answers because some sacred book or guru tells them so. That kind of secondhand thinking, where you put your mind to sleep and just download someone else's ideas through a pipe into the jelly of your brain, is unworthy of a genuine human being. Anyone too lazy to think does not deserve to know any of the answers.

**AJF**: Thank you so much again for taking the time to chat with DD. Please tell our readers the best place to find more of your work online.

**RT**: My books *The Sphinx Mystery* and *Egyptian Dawn* have extensive and elaborate dedicated websites containing all the illustrations plus additional ones, and their web addresses are: www.sphinxmystery. com and www.egyptiandawn. com. My translation of Rainer Maria Rilke's book of poetry *Sonnets to Orpheus* has its own dedicated website, which is www. sonnetstoorpheus.com. My earlier books do not have dedicated websites of their own, but I do intend to do one for *The Sirius Mystery* some time at www.siriusmystery.com,

and my new book will have one at www.newscienceofheaven.com.

My personal website is www.robert-temple.com and you have to add the hyphen (dash) between robert and temple, because there is a dentist or someone who has a website for roberttemple. My website contains a large number of things I have written and published over the years, and many which I never published at all. (Click on Bibliography to find many of these, and there are numerous unpublished tales I have to tell under NOSTALGIA, such as my memories of Joan Rivers, Tallulah Bankhead, Huntington Hartford, and so forth.) And if anyone is interested in movies, if you click on MY FILM REVIEWS at the top of my website home page, you will find all of my 1,051 film reviews so far for the website www.IMDb.com and many of those are of very rare films, as I have a passion for cinema history, film noir, foreign language films, and also dog films, for I am a dog-lover and will watch any dog film with great enthusiasm (try watching *Underdog* if you want to die laughing). The film review list comes up as chronological, but if you click on Alphabetical, you can search alphabetically for any particular favorite film to see if I have reviewed it. Many of my film reviews are a thousand words long (the maximum permitted) and the total I have written are thus coming perilously close to amounting to about a million words!

My 95-page technical paper on quantum theory, published in 2016, may be found on the website of The Journal of Cosmology (Volume 25, Number 3, pp. 13995-14090). Its title is "Is Particle Mass a Function of Degrees of Freedom?" It contains numerous original formulae, such as for the mass of the proton and other such things of a rarefied nature, which will only make sense to people familiar with advanced physics, hence it is of no interest to the general public at all. ◗

# CLOSE TO THE NEWS

BY ROBERT K. G. TEMPLE

It was the habit of the Griffiths to watch the news every evening on television. They kept no fixed times, for in the winter they tended to watch earlier because it got dark earlier, and in the summer they might be quite late sitting down to see what was happening in the world. They therefore tended to watch the 24-hour channels, as they never knew when they might want to see the news. Gone were the days when the terrestrial channels broadcast the news only at fixed times, and if you missed it, you had to wait till next day. Now it was there all the time, although it was very repetitive, because they kept saying the same thing over and over again every half hour. Sometimes one sat in more or less of a stupor allowing repetition to drift partially into one's awareness, while thinking of other things. And sometimes one was alert enough to turn it off.

Alice Griffiths was 14 and discovering the world about her with the ardent determination of someone awakening. And so she watched the news eagerly. She had realized there was a world out there, and all she had to do was sit and watch the news in order learn what was happening in it. She became fascinated with all of those remote countries where people never stopped bombing and killing one another, so many of which had all those concrete buildings which seemed to have been built solely to be turned into rubble to be seen on the news. Other of the countries seemed to consist of huts and endless countryside with mud roads, and men sitting on strange vehicles with huge machine guns on top. Sometimes also men with guns wore masks over their faces. Alice began to realize that there were lots of killers on the loose throughout the world, and she was very lucky not to live in one of those places where the only thing that seemed to happen was violent death.

Alice's parents were pleased that she was taking an interest in world affairs, and they would sometimes exchange pleased glances with one another when she was not looking, thinking how proud they were to have such a clever daughter.

Something strange which Alice's parents noticed about her, however, was that Alice did not chatter about what she had seen on the news. They had expected her to be more talkative, but instead she seemed to take and keep the news inward, not letting it out. It was as if she were making the news a part of her, absorbing it into herself, and refusing to let it out again. Her parents often wondered what she thought of all the things she saw on the news, but they did not wish to probe, and as she did not volunteer her thoughts, they respected the seriousness with which she seemed to wish to brood on them silently.

They were surprised when Alice moved her chair much closer to the television set one day, and left it there from then on. It made them uncomfortable to think of anyone sitting that close to the screen, but they said nothing.

Often Alice appeared to have a faraway look in her eye, on those occasions when they ate together. Of course, when Alice's parents were young, it was considered both normal and necessary for families to sit and have meals together. Alice did this from time to time, in a desultory and inattentive manner. It was then that her parents had the opportunity to watch her face closely, without appearing to want to study her expression or look at her abstracted eyes which were not focused on them.

If they commented upon the potatoes, Alice could answer normally in an automatic manner and keep the conversation going, without however altering her gaze into space. They knew she didn't like peas, so they never served any to her or mentioned them, even though they were very keen on them themselves, and had them frequently amongst the dishes on the table at supper. Alice put the potatoes and other food in her mouth without really looking directly at her fork. She could even cut meat without focusing on the task.

One evening, Alice said at supper:

'I don't like tanks. They are horrid.'

This was so out of context with enjoying a really good meal that her parents were nonplussed and replied quietly with murmurs of agreement. Alice's mother emphasized the common spirit by saying: 'Yes, horrid!'

Alice did not comment further or say anything else for the rest of the meal.

She never had breakfast with her parents during the week, but if they waited for her to wake up late, they could all have breakfast together on Saturdays. And one Saturday she said suddenly: 'I can't keep up with all the wars. And they don't keep up coverage of them all on the news in suitably continuous manner. They shift from war to war all the time, and I wonder what is going on in one war still when they have become more interested in the next one. I want to know about all the wars all the time. But they won't do that.'

Mr. and Mrs. Griffiths thought it best to say nothing, not even to murmur in agreement or make sympathetic noises; they just remained silent.

Alice announced one day that she wanted to go to the television news studio of a particular channel that she liked. But when her parents told her that as it was France 24, and the studio must be in Paris, she became very angry, and then lapsed into a depressed silence. They tried to steer her away from this subject by mentioning that they were going to Sainsbury's and which ice cream did she fancy this time. But she failed to answer. So they bought butter pecan and hoped for the best. It was a bit too American for their tastes, but they knew she liked it. She seemed pleased, although she did not mention it.

But Mr. and Mrs. Griffiths became alarmed when that evening, with her bowl of butter pecan ice cream on her lap, Alice moved her chair even closer to the television. They really thought it would be bad for her eyes, but they said nothing. 'Would you like me to take your bowl, darling?' asked her mother. Alice held it out without comment for her mother to take, absorbed as she was in watching a report about the arrests of some people who might be terrorists because they had laughed at a policeman. They were strip-searched, but nothing was found, so the report claimed that their homes had been searched and their computers seized in order to find the evidence of their connections with other terrorists.

Mr. and Mrs. Griffiths would have liked to watch a popular entertainment programme, but they did not dare to suggest it. They were tired of the news all the time, but Alice appeared never to tire of it.

A few weeks later, worn out by Alice's addiction, her parents were so exasperated that they whispered together about how to express to Alice their frustration at missing various variety shows on television, which were their favourites, as well as some wildlife documentaries which they also liked. Mr. Griffiths was not in agreement with his wife that they should buy a separate television for their daughter's bedroom, where she could watch what she wanted and they could watch what they wanted. He thought it would increase her sense of isolation and break up the family spirit in the household. His wife, at the end of her tether, reluctantly agreed, but asked him what then he suggested they should do. Mr. Griffiths said they must begin trying to formulate how they would politely phrase their position without alienating their daughter and causing her to feel oppressed by dictatorial parents, which was the great dread of all the other parents whom they knew, who were all being blackmailed by their children into getting what they wanted by threats of withdrawal of filial affection and the destruction of the family harmony.

Alice's parents were secretly rehearsing what they would say to Alice and how they would say it, hoping to keep her goodwill, when they noticed that it was near bedtime and Alice appeared to have nodded off in front of the television set, sitting in her chair far in front of them. They could see that her head had lolled down onto her shoulder and she was clearly dozing. They were relieved that they could now turn the news off. So Mrs. Griffith turned off the TV with the remote control and was about to tiptoe away to get a glass of water in the kitchen before going silently up to bed with her husband, leaving their daughter to doze peacefully and undisturbed.

However, Mrs. Griffiths was puzzled that despite having turned off the TV, she still appeared to hear the sound of the news broadcast continuing very faintly somehow. She looked at her husband, and they exchanged puzzled glances, and got up to go quietly over to Alice to see what could possibly be happening, and how this was possible.

As they approached Alice, who was clearly asleep, the sound of the news broadcast became slightly louder. The sound actually appeared to be coming from Alice herself. So they assumed that she must be holding some device in her hand. They gently raised her head from her shoulder and arranged it straight, as they were concerned she might wake up with a crook in her neck. Then they looked down at her hands, but she was holding nothing, and her hands were limp.

Where was the sound coming from? They were mystified.

Next they went over to inspect the TV set. But it was definitely turned off, with a red light showing, and the sound was not coming from it. No, the sound was coming from Alice, not the TV.

Having looked at her lap again, and having found nothing, their attention was drawn to Alice's face. They started violently at the same time when they both noticed that her eyes were open and not shut. And there was a strange flickering about them. They came closer and saw that flickering light seemed to be coming from her eyes. They peered more closely still, and were so shocked, they were for an instant paralyzed with astonishment. They could not believe what they were seeing. But within a few instants, they took it in. There was no mistaking it, although they could not understand it. In each open eye of their sleeping daughter, they could see the news broadcast which they had turned off. It was continuing somehow, and it could be viewed by looking closely into Alice's eyes. The sound was coming from her, just as the image was being broadcast by her own eyes.

Mrs. Griffith screamed loudly, but the news did not stop. Another bombing incident was being reported, and she could see the face of the news reader in miniature, in Alice's open eyes. Mrs. Griffiths screamed and screamed and screamed. Alice did not wake up. Mr. and Mrs. Griffiths looked with horror at their daughter. But the news continued without interruption, as is the way with 24-hour news. ◉

## Sam Hunter is a PI in the big bad city

When he takes a new case it's like he's accepting the client into his 'pack'. And Sam will do anything to protect the members of his pack. Dogs are like that. So are wolves. And so, too, are werewolves. Like Sam.

Sam is a benandanti, an ancient race of werewolves who fight evil. And evil comes in all shapes and sizes; it comes at people from all directions. The cases Sam takes range from saving the world from genetically-engineered super soldiers to saving a young boy from the very real monster in his closet.

The Sam Hunter Case Files gather together the weird, strange, funny, heartbreaking and disturbing adventures of a low-rent private investigator taking on very odd jobs. These stories include cameos by fan-favorite characters from Maberry's bestselling Joe Ledger thrillers and The Pine Deep Trilogy.

# RELEASES FROM JONATHAN MABERRY

Tales of horror, suspense, adventure and mystery take readers to the troubled little town of Pine Deep, to the feudal Japan of the Samurai, to the angry red planet of John Carter of Mars, and elsewhere.

WWW.JOURNALSTONE.COM

# THE RUN OF THE TOWN

## BY RAMSEY CAMPBELL

Cramp wakened Plater before dawn. He sprawled out of bed and lurched stiff-legged around the hotel room, ending up at the window. As he gripped the sill so hard his nails bent while he stretched out his leg in the hope of diminishing the pain, he glimpsed activity in the distance. Beyond ranks of grey roofs descending a hill a park was dimly lit by streetlamps. The pale glow outlined a statue at the junction of several paths, and when he strained his eyes Plater made out joggers in the park. Perhaps they were keeping fit for

the hilly streets, though he would have thought the streets themselves might keep them trim. The cramp had subsided to a dull ache, and he limped back to bed.

He hadn't planned to spend the night away from home. Helping Carol unload her belongings at the university – such a carload that it had left no space for her mother – had taken hours longer than he'd anticipated. On the drive home he'd met a downpour so relentless that he could see no more than a few yards ahead. Though the fog of spray failed

to slow the traffic, several accidents did, and once he was reduced to crawling little more than a mile in an hour he'd followed an exit sign he could scarcely read. He'd left the rain and the daylight behind by the time he found the hotel at the edge of Chalmerston, a small steep grey Derbyshire town. He didn't think he'd seen the name on the motorway sign, but just then he couldn't have imagined a more welcome sight than the hotel car park.

A twinge of cramp roused him from dozing. A blob of sunlight

mushroomed in the clotted greyish sky above the jagged horizon. Plater used the shower, which suffered from an intermittent chilly stutter, and took the lift down to the basement. As he collected items from the breakfast buffet – enough to last him all the way home without a break – several greying couples bade him a muted English morning. He was back in his room when he thought of walking before driving, not least to work out the last persistent trace of cramp. He brushed his teeth with the flimsy instrument the hotel provided,

and was crossing the lobby when the hotel receptionist, a squat broad long-faced man, halted him with a frown. "Leaving us already?"

"Just going for a walk first." Plater felt sufficiently accused to add "I'll settle up now if you like."

"No call for that. We've got you written down." The man tapped the computer screen in front of him, which emitted a pinched clink. "Not here for the chase, then," he said.

"I can't say I am."

The man raised his head, which seemed both to lengthen his face and

intensify his disapproval. "You're one of them who'd like it stopped, are you?"

"I might if I knew what it was. If we're talking about hunting, surely that's banned."

"We leave the wild life to itself round here. It can't help what it gets up to, not like you and me."

"Then I'm honestly lost. What were you thinking I should know?"

"You've got a way with words and no mistake." The frown squeezed the comment dry of any trace of praise. "Best thing might be," the receptionist said, "the world forgets about us."

"You aren't still talking about you and me."

"I'm talking about history some interfering buggers want to do away with."

"I hope you don't think I'm one of those. I've just dropped off my daughter who's studying history."

"I'd not like to say what I think. The way they teach history these days..." With a breath fierce enough to do duty as an observation the receptionist said "Tradition, that's what they want to get rid of."

"I really don't think that's altogether the case. Will you have met many lecturers yourself?"

"Meddlers." Apparently to clarify, the man said "The ones who want to try and take away our character."

Plater had to assume "Of your town."

"It's been three hundred years and more, and the town's getting on for that too. That's when they started mining far side of the hill."

"And before that..." When the man didn't answer, Plater said "What was more than three hundred years back?"

"The real chase, and if you ask me it did none of them much harm. If they hadn't lived round here they might have come off a lot worse." The man's head jerked as though he'd wakened from a reverie. "Any road," he said, "you'll be wanting your walk."

Plater might have enquired further if the phone on the counter hadn't rung. As he made for the street the glass door crept aside for him. On his way downhill he had to step into the road to avoid an aproned butcher who was hauling out an awning with a hook. Otherwise the street was deserted except for a large whitish dog that fell to all fours from nosing in a bin and fled along an alley at Plater's approach. Ahead he saw the river to which the streets led down both sides of the valley – water that the sky turned a grey like the colour of sluggishness – but he was heading for the park.

Or was it a park? Perhaps it once had been. When he located the entrance, having followed a hedge twice his height and so impenetrably tangled that it wasn't much less solid than a wall, he found the gates were padlocked. Through the rusty iron bars, which were as spiky as the hedge, he saw that the place must have been abandoned quite a while ago, since the weedy grass between the trees had grown taller than him. Nevertheless the area was still in use, perhaps only by intruders. The tracks he'd mistaken for ordinary paths last night had been forced through the vegetation, to judge by the only one leading away from the entrance – from a gap in the hedge beside the lichened pillar that supported the left-hand gate.

The gap was barely wide enough for him to sidle through. Perhaps children had originally made it, breaking off the twigs that were strewn outside the hedge, and the joggers he'd seen were sufficiently thin to fit. He clenched himself to slimness so as not to be scratched by the thorns, because he was interested in visiting what he'd seen from the hotel window, not to mention the large house that his vantage point had hidden. Encountering so many students yesterday had left him feeling old and unadventurous. Once he would have been eager to explore a place like this, and he could think of no reason not to feel that way still.

Whoever had trampled the grass seemed to have been in no hurry to arrive at the house, for the sodden brownish path took quite a devious route among the trees. Well before he reached the statue Plater crossed several other tracks, which wandered maze-like out of sight through the grass. They appeared to converge on the statue, which was encircled by a wider patch of trodden vegetation. He was close to the weathered figure before he noticed that it and its companions had their backs to him.

They faced the house, where planks were nailed across the lofty front door and every visible window was boarded up. The eroded statues bristled with wads of moss, and the central figure's face had sloughed away like fungus. The features of both of the heads on which its hands rested had fallen off as well, and Plater couldn't imagine what expressions they might have borne as the pair of figures stooped forward. No doubt the stance was meant to acknowledge the touch of their benefactor, however much they resembled runners awaiting the start of a race. Having searched in vain for names – not even the main figure was identified – Plater made for the house.

Five windows flanked each side of the pillared porch, and a solitary trampled path led to the nearest left-hand window, from which a board had been wrenched loose. The pane was smashed as well, and through the gap he could just distinguish a room so large that the muffled sunlight fell short of most of it. As his eyes adjusted to the dimness he saw an indistinct reflection of the statue in a mirror across the room. The gap between the boards was so narrow that it would take somebody thinner than him to clamber through, and in any case that seemed more foolhardy than adventurous. Instead he leaned against a scaly flaking pillar of the porch and used his phone to search for Chalmerston.

It had been a miners' town until the industry exploded into conflict in the eighties. After the mine was shut down, Chalmerston had become a centre for walkers in the countryside. The Wikipedia entry made no mention of any kind of chase, and Plater wondered if whoever the receptionist had accused of trying to end the tradition could have edited the article. As a breeze made the broken pane whistle, a sound so thin it might have been issuing between teeth, he tried looking up Chalmerston Chase. It was an annual event, a May Day run through the town, all the way from the top to the bottom and up the other side. May Day was nearly a week hence, but Plater didn't know if he would have enjoyed the spectacle of competitors exerting themselves so much. Apparently the event was called Chalmer's Chase, and as Plater searched for further information he tried to ignore the attenuated whistling, which sounded as though it was inside the house. There was indeed a campaign to end the tradition, not least because former miners from nearby towns thought it offensive to celebrate a workers' holiday with an event based on the exploitation of their counterparts centuries ago. By now Plater was certain that somebody was whistling between their teeth and calling in a low voice to a dog. How had people been exploited round here in the past? Another online reference established that the event had originally been known as Charmer's Chase, named for a bygone dignitary and landowner, Justice Charmer – quite possibly, Plater thought, the former owner of the ruined mansion. Had Justice been his name or his calling or both? Supposedly he'd pardoned local criminals so long as they took an oath to guard his property – "to chase away the inquisitive", though the reason was left undefined. Between toothy whistles the man somewhere nearby was still calling the dog, which was presumably able to hear even such a low voice. In fact, there must be more than one, though would anybody give dogs such names except as a joke? "Walker... Hunt... Hill..." A final online link questioned the view of Charmer as benevolent, suggesting that he contrived to find too many of the tenants of the farms and cottages on his land guilty of some offence in order to increase the patrol, and that he'd hold them to their vow even once they'd reached an age that seemed unreasonable if not positively unnatural. If this or any other aspect of his behaviour had eventually provoked a reaction, it seemed to be nowhere on the record, much like the end of Justice Charmer. Perhaps the voice was distant, not muffled, and could its owner be calling his employees to a job? "Hall... Wood... Stone..." The words needn't even be

the names of people; perhaps they related to some renovation of the house, and the reiterated whistle might be an inadvertent mannerism. Plater's wanderings online had just prompted a random thought – that charmer was another word for wizard – when the phone twitched in his hand.

The bell was as shrill as the whistling. He had an irrational fancy that he'd attracted the call with his online search, even when he read the caller's name. As he raised the phone to speak it said "Pater."

The word threw him so much that he demanded "What are you saying?"

"Only teasing, dad. My roommate calls hers that. I was only calling to say thank you for being – "

He had to believe he'd misheard Carol's last word. "Being dad, you said."

"What else would I have? You're not driving, are you? You sound a bit distracted."

"I will be. Driving, that's to say. The traffic was so wretched I stayed somewhere overnight."

"Then don't let me stop you getting back to mum. Have a good run and I'll call you when you're free."

As Plater put away his mobile he heard the whistle and the voice. He found it even harder to determine how far away the fellow was, though he seemed to be calling for a painter. Despite his eagerness to set off for home, Plater went back to the broken window. The only figure to be seen was the reflection in the mirror, and it occurred to him that the statue might have been situated so that the owner of the house could see his own image from any of the front rooms. Leafy shadows on the statue lent restless movements to the dim discoloured shape across the room. A trick of light or of perspective obscured its companions, so that Plater might have imagined that the outstretched hands were resting on emptiness – in fact, that they were lifted higher and extended further than the ones behind him. He swung around to see that there were no shadows on

the statue, just patches of moss. He hadn't time or any wish to think why he made at some speed for the path to the gates.

He could still hear the man calling out names. Perhaps one of them was Painter, not anybody's job after all. Even once the statue was behind him Plater could still hear the low voice. When he reached the track through the grass the sounds of his progress began to blot out the calls, until the rustling around him grew so insistent that he could have imagined he wasn't alone. No doubt a wind was responsible for this and for keeping the voice after him. Of course only vegetation was on the move along the paths he crossed, and he focused his attention on the gates. While easing himself through the hedge he noticed once again that all the snapped-off twigs lay outside the grounds of the mansion, as if the gap had been forced open from within.

His cramp had threatened to return on the path, and his leg kept giving a reminiscent twitch as he tramped uphill. Nearby somebody was whistling, a practice that a fast food chain had brought back into fashion, though this whistler stopped at one note. More shops were open, and one that bore a tobacconist's vintage sign exhibited a placard for the *Chalmerston Champion*, declaring that this year's chase would go ahead. He'd left it well behind when he heard somebody selling the paper, unless they were announcing a delivery of one. It wasn't in this street; a backwards glance showed him no sign of the paper. The shout had made his leg jerk, at the mercy of a nerve, and he did his best to limber it up as he climbed to the hotel.

He was regaining his breath when the receptionist came out of the office behind the counter. "Had your run, have you?"

"I wouldn't call. It that." Once he could utter an uninterrupted sentence Plater said "I think I found where your chase began."

Perhaps the man was as exhausted as Plater felt, since he seemed to need to sit down. "Where are you saying?"

"The big old ruin near the river. That's Charmer's statue down there, isn't it? I couldn't see its name."

"Who said you could go in there? It's all locked up."

"Someone was jogging there last night, or maybe they were practicing for your event."

The receptionist stared as though suppressing a response. "Thought you didn't want to stir things up."

"I'm not sure how you think I – "

"The lot that want to stop it did," the receptionist said and turned to the computer.

As the man muttered at the screen Plater caught his own name. "I'm sorry, what did you say to me?"

"I'm saying you've got your stay with us to pay for."

"I was about to. I just hadn't heard you ask."

The receptionist scrutinised the credit card at such length that Plater could have thought he was going to read out the name. When the machine protruded a paper tongue the man tore it off and enfolded the card in it so thoroughly that the act looked almost ritualistic. "Hope you find your way," he said and retreated into the office.

Plater was at the glass door, though apparently not close enough to trigger the mechanism, when he thought he heard his name. His leg gave an inadvertent jerk before he realised he must have overheard something else. It was surely too early for anyone to be asking for a chaser in the bar. No doubt the voice was in the breakfast room; he'd sounded subterranean, the man ordering a plate of whatever it had been. Plater lurched at the door, which crept aside at last, and limped to his car.

He leaned on the roof and flexed his leg while he called Dorothy. He'd spoken to her last night, but now she wasn't at home. The message she'd recorded years ago promised that one of them would call back later. A trick of the connection emphasised their last name and her final word. "Just

Sam," he said, "setting off right now," and lowered himself into the car.

A pointer opposite the exit from the car park sent him downhill. He turned left at the first cross street, since there was no entry to the right-hand stretch. He meant to turn uphill as soon as he could, returning to the road that had brought him to Chalmerston. The street he reached was one way too, and he had to drive downhill until a right turn led him back to the street he'd started from. When he crossed it, a series of one-way streets that might almost have been a mirror image of the route he'd just followed took him to the junction where he'd turned left in the first place.

The way out of town must be further downhill. As he drove past the tobacconist's he thought he heard the call about the paper once again, and his leg gave an involuntary twitch. He could only turn left at the next crossroads, where the opposite street didn't admit traffic. The route led downwards and then right, crossing the street that contained the hotel before directing him through another series of grey stone terraces, so similar to those he'd already encountered that it felt like a repetition. It certainly resembled his previous route, given how it contrived to bring him back to the junction nearest the hotel.

He swung the car downhill at once, with a screech of brakes piercing enough for a whistle. Somewhere nearby a teacher was announcing playtime at a school, though Plater would have thought they'd use a bell. There was only one more crossroads, and the noise of the brakes made his leg twitch. Yet again he could only turn left, but the one-way street at the end of the terrace of grey houses descended straight to the foot of the hill – to the road alongside the grounds of the ruined mansion.

A pointer – he could have imagined that he was hearing the word, though surely only in his head – sent him past the mansion. Presumably there was a sports field on the far side of town,

since somebody beyond the hedge was exhorting people to play to win, though Plater missed the last word. His leg jerked and the brakes whined high as he turned uphill, having found a street that would admit the car. He was almost prepared to find himself back at the highest junction, in which case he meant to park wherever he could and ask for directions at the hotel. But when the route forced him to follow a street across the slope, it returned him to the road closest to the mansion.

How distracted had he let himself become? Why hadn't he thought of using the map? When he brought up the town on his phone, however, it showed no trace of the one-way system. This only helped the streets to put him in mind of a maze – of the paths through the grass – and staring at the image made parts of it appear to darken, not least some of the letters spelling the town: a, l, e, r, t… Plater meant to be, though he was troubled by the notion that they could form other words: alter, later. He dropped the phone on the seat next to him and drove down to the lowest road, passing the unseen mansion before he took another uphill route. Unrelieved ranks of grey stone houses shut him in and sent him right, and right again. When he reached a crossroads he was desperate to believe he hadn't previously met it, but there was the mansion again, lying in wait at the bottom of the hill.

The streets weren't deserted. There were people he could ask. One was labouring downhill towards him: a woman with a toddler in a pushchair and a small girl beside them. It was plain that rotundity ran in the family, and the woman and the girl might have been striving not to jog, proceeding at a slowness meant to counteract the effect of the slope. Plater lowered his window as the plodding party came abreast of him. "Excuse me, which way for the motorway?"

The woman's voice was as dull as her sluggish blink. "Way for?"

"Wafer," the girl said to her little brother, so low that Plater might have mistaken the word.

"Which way to it, I'm asking."

"Way to?"

Plater felt not much less confused than she appeared to be. He was disconcerted by observing that the toddler had a chewed plastic whistle in his mouth. Carol would never have had such an item at that age; they were too easily swallowed. "Wafer," the girl murmured, or a similar word.

Was she playing a game, perhaps a local one? "The way out," Plater told the woman while he tried to quell the jerking of his leg. "The way out of town."

"Outer," the girl muttered, if not something else, as her mother said "How did you get in?"

"On the road that comes to the hotel at the top."

"Better go the other way, then."

"Other," the girl mumbled – at least, Plater thought he heard that – and the toddler's face puffed up as he blew the whistle with unexpected strength.

The sound felt as if it was penetrating Plater's body, and made his foot jerk on the accelerator. "Thanks," he said and was driving downhill almost before he could choose to do so. The woman might have helped, however perfunctory her advice had been. If he must leave Chalmerston by the far side, at least he would be escaping the town. Once he reached the open countryside there would be signs to show him the way home.

He turned right when the clawed hedge rose above him, and drove past the mansion it hid. It ended at a junction, one branch of which led behind the building to a bridge across the river, while on this side of the water both roads climbed the hill. He could see how they became entangled in the one-way system, but the road beyond the bridge led straight to the top and over the hill. He swung the car onto the bridge at once.

A waterfowl emitted a piercing note as he passed over, a noise he found difficult to put out of his head. He tried switching on the radio, which brought him a local station; certainly the man sounded local. Was he saying he would pray for someone or, surely likelier, announcing a record he was about to play for a listener? No doubt the whistle was the start of the track, but it made Plater's leg twitch, and he turned the radio off. He needed to concentrate, because the hill was so steep that he could imagine the grey houses toppling down it like dominoes – so steep that he had to change to a lower gear. No wonder some people at the top were descending at such a speed, several of them on both pavements. They would be joggers, however helplessly precipitous their progress looked – in fact, so haphazard and beyond their control that they were spilling off the pavements into the road. Couldn't they see his car, or did they expect him to accommodate them? Admittedly they had the street to themselves; everybody else must be staying inside the houses or out of the way elsewhere. The runners were racing towards him faster than the car was climbing, and he could have thought they were unaware of him, especially since their heads were lowered, which went with their crouching stance. There were at least a dozen of them, and as Plater changed to second gear they spread across the road, blocking his way entirely despite how thin they all were. He leaned on the horn, and they lifted their heads in unison, revealing far too much. They were already close enough for him to see that their clothes were ragged and discoloured, but so was the rest of them, not least their faces: the frayed gaping lips, the eyes like blobs of dried mud. Now he saw that they were mouthing in chorus, "play too" or a name or both. They were almost upon him, and he thought of driving straight through them, but the car was still losing impetus. He swerved with a screech of brakes that might have covered up another high sound and sent the car speeding off the main road.

He'd thought he was driving into a side street, but it was no more than an alley. In fact, the high blank walls on both sides were closing in, and he wasn't halfway to the next street when they began to scrape the housing of the wing mirrors. As he fumbled to lower the window beside him so that he could drag the mirror against the car, he glimpsed figures swarming into the alley behind him. The alley was growing narrower still, and if he drove much further he would simply jam the bonnet between the walls. In a panic that swept away most of his thoughts he opened the door while he still could – at the entrance to another alley – and fled downhill.

The mansion rose towards him as though it had all the time in the world. He would have dodged aside if he could, but the alley led straight down without a break in either wall. Plater felt as if the jerking of his leg was compelling him to jog faster. Echoes of his footsteps, shrill as whistling, boxed him in. He heard scrabbling and scrawny thuds behind him as pursuers made their various ways past or over the car. The slope seemed to be forcing him into a crouch that brought his head low, and he was so intent on not glancing back that he only belatedly noticed the figure that was waiting for him. He would have liked to think it was a statue, because surely only stone could make the costume so indistinguishable from its wearer and from the lichen that blotched the crumbling form. But when it pressed Plater's head down, its hand was colder than stone. ⚫

# WHAT THE HELL EVER HAPPENED TO...

# JOHN COYNE

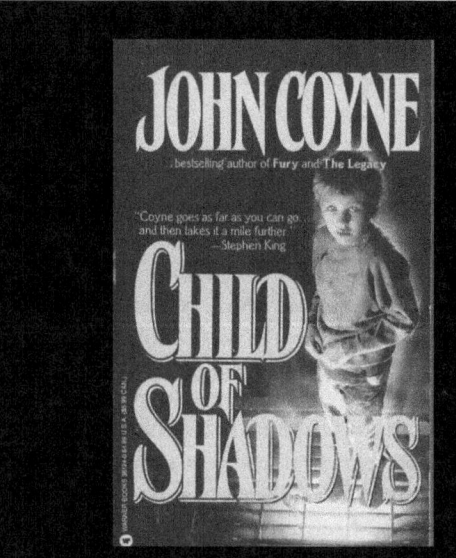   

BY ROBERT MORRISH

John Coyne is the author of 13 published novels, eight of which qualify as horror, the last of which appeared in 1990. Right from the beginning of his career, Coyne threatened to become one of the major writers of the horror genre, on a level with King, Koontz, and Straub, but never quite managed to reach those peaks. His achievements are still pretty impressive, though, for someone who grew up wanting to be a professional golfer, wrote six unpublished novels before selling his seventh, and considers writing to be roughly his sixth "career."

Coyne attended St. Louis University for his undergraduate work and Western Michigan University for grad school, and served two stints in the Peace Corps. He also worked for the government and acted as the dean of a college before deciding to become a full-time writer in 1971. In addition to honing his novel-writing skills during the next few years, he published several nonfiction titles on alternative education, and found success selling short fiction to *Alfred Hitchcock's Mystery Magazine* and *Ellery Queen's Mystery Magazine*.

Despite the extensive preliminaries, Coyne nonetheless seemed to burst onto the horror scene in 1979 with his first two published books, *The Piercing* (Putnam, 1979), and his novelization of the film *The Legacy* (Berkley, 1979). Hardcover rights for *The Piercing* sold to Putnam, with a significant advance from Berkeley for the paperback rights. In the interim, Berkley asked Coyne to write a novelization for *The Legacy*, which he did in three weeks. The plot of *The Legacy* concerns six people who are invited to the remote home of a dying millionaire, who promises to make one of them heir to his wealth and power. In the style of "Ten Little Indians," they then begin to die, one by one. The movie opened and closed with barely a whimper, but the novelization of *The Legacy* went on to sell more than two million copies, and the market was primed for the subsequent publication of the paperback edition of *The Piercing*, which centers on a young woman whose clockwork manifestation of stigmata on a weekly basis earns her a spotlight in the media, but only derision from organized religion. A single priest believes that the effects are genuine, but that they are caused by demonic forces.

Coyne's next two books, *The Searing* (Putnam, 1980) and *Hobgoblin* (Putnam, 1981) also didn't produce big numbers in hardcover, but sold like hotcakes in their paperback editions. *The Searing* features a unique plot: in a small village, every woman in town simultaneously experiences a moment of orgasmic pleasure each night, but at the same time, local infants are dying. The key to it all seems to be one particular autistic child. *Hobgoblin*, meanwhile, concerns a teenaged boy who's addicted to the titular role-playing game, and whose stability is further eroded by a series of traumatic events: the unexpected death of his father, moving with his mother to an old Irish mansion that's been rebuilt on the Hudson River, and the accompanying move to a new high school where he's scorned and bullied.

As a result of the respective hardcover/paperback sales numbers for *The Searing* and *Hobgoblin*, Coyne's next novel, *The Shroud* (Berkley, 1983) went straight to paperback. The novel in-

volves disappearances of the homeless in New York, and a young priest who has reason to believe that the disappearances are caused by supernatural events that he's linked to.

At this point in his career, the author made an attempt to escape the confines of the horror genre, publishing *Brothers and Sisters* (1986), a family saga about an Irish immigrant with an IRA past. But market forces then compelled Coyne to return to horror with *The Hunting Season* (Macmillan, 1987), in which a recently wed young woman moves to a remote community

where she attempts an anthropological study of the local ingrown culture, only to uncover far more bizarre secrets, including mutants living in the woods and a form of communal madness. Next came *Fury* (Warner, 1989), which centers on a young woman who appears on the surface to be extremely intelligent, attractive, and upwardly mobile, but who hides a dark secret: when angered, she displays brutal ferocity, the result of her being the reincarnation of an ancient hunter.

Finally, Coyne delivered *Child of Shadows* (Warner, 1990), involving a

world-weary social worker who rescues a feral child living in the New York subway system and moves him to a remote town in North Carolina, where the locals don't appreciate the newcomers, and a series of murders and mutilations cast suspicion on them. Like most of Coyne's work, *Child of Shadows* was well-received critically, with Publishers Weekly saying: "The real interest of *Child of Shadows* lies not only in the twists and turns of the plot, but also in the exploration of Melissa's psychological history."

Despite the relative critical and commercial success he'd received, Coyne largely walked away from horror after that novel, with only a few subsequent short stories in the genre. In later years, he's written three novels that revolve around golfing, and his most recent, a mainstream novel (*Long Ago and Far Away:* A love story, which appeared in 2014), as well as some nonfiction titles.

Finally, it's worth noting that this interview will appear "just in time" for Coyne to still be considered a legitimate candidate for a column entitled "What the Hell Ever Happened To...?", as his comeback in the horror genre is imminent—he has a collection, tentatively titled *The Devil You Know and Other Tales of Terror*, due in late 2017 from Cemetery Dance Publications.

**Dark Discoveries:** You've referred to yourself as someone who knows the business of publishing more than someone who's a prose stylist or a writer's writer. Talk a little bit about that, if you will...

**John Coyne:** It's probably because I married a book editor, and book editors only hang around with other book editors, and I've had that perspective to watch things change over the years... I've had about five agents over the years, and I've written 26 books, with the last two being self-published books. The whole industry has changed.

What I tell anybody who's interested in writing a book is that there are three aspects to it. Number one is you have to come up with an idea; number two, you have to write the idea; and three, you have to sell the book. So there are three different skills involved. You have to be able to do all of those things in order to make it work.

**DD:** *The Piercing* was the seventh novel you had written, but the first you published. Tell us a little about those first six unpublished books, and about the patience and dedication it took to continue writing in those early days when you weren't meeting with much success.

**JC:** The first one was called *A Cool Breeze For Evening*, and that was set in Africa. It was a book that was basically a Peace Corps volunteer remembering what had happened to him during his two years as a volunteer. But they were mostly suspense stories. They were not horror, or supernatural, at all. They were really books that, if you had to classify them, you'd probably call them adventure/suspense novels. I only have one of them left now, since they were all written pre-computer. I did write some early short stories that do fit into the genre, and many of them are being reprinted in the Cemetery Dance collection.

If you track my career, you can see I've had to patchwork things together, like 99% of most writers do, in order to keep writing. Early on, I wrote a couple of non-fiction books, including a book called *This Way Out: A Guide to Alternative Education*, because I was working as a dean at a college. So, those helped, at least in terms of giving me a credit as being able to write a book, and I made some contacts. And I also made my first commercial short story sale, which I believe was with *Ellery Queen's Mystery Magazine*.

And then I remember reading *Carrie* when it came out, and thinking to myself, "I could do this." I just needed

to come up with an idea, so I came up with the idea of stigmata, which was the seed for *The Piercing*. I was able to work in a lot of the stuff that I was raised with in the Catholic faith. And the book sort of just took off. But the reason it took off was the time—King had sort of caught everybody's eye, and created an appetite for horror.

**DD:** You've made a point in previous interviews about how books sell through word of mouth and advertising, and how unimportant the author's name can actually be, pointing out the small print in which your name appears on some of your books' covers. Could you recap those feelings for *Dark Discoveries'* readers?

**JC:** Well, certainly when you're first starting to get published, readers won't say "have you read that Coyne book?," they'll say "have you read *The Piercing*?" Of course, once you become more of a household name, that changes. Today, someone wouldn't ask "have you read [*End of Watch*]?," they'd ask, "have you read the new Stephen King book?"

**DD:** It's been said that you purposely styled *The Piercing* after *The Exorcist*, which had been so wildly successful. Is that fair to say?

**JC:** Not really... They're similar only in the sense that both center on a priest involved with a young woman who's going through a "mystical experience." *The Exorcist* was set in Washington, D.C., while I set my book in North Carolina, because I'd spent some time down there working on a couple of non-fiction books... and it was so different there from what I knew from living elsewhere, that I felt it was the perfect, remote type of setting for a story like that. And then I decided to structure the story around the forty days of Lent, which was great, because it gave me the structure I needed to write the book.

**DD:** Your novelization of *The Legacy* was written in three weeks—what was that experience like? Were you work-

ing strictly from a script, or was a cut of the film available for screening?

**JC:** At the time, I'd finished *The Piercing*, and I was over in Spain and I got a telegram from my editor, asking me to call Putnam. Putnam at that time was owned by Universal Studios, and they'd just had a huge success with a novelization they'd published, so they decided they wanted to promote [the film version of] *The Legacy* in the same way. So I came back and I met with them, and they said, "Can you do it? And can you do it in three weeks?"

They gave me the script, and that was it. I asked for still photos of various parts of the movie, which I understand really pissed them off, because they had to spend the money for that. I never saw the film until after book was published.

**DD:** I believe you've stated that *The Searing* was somewhat inspired by the nonfiction bestseller, Chariots of the Gods... tell us more about how *The Searing* came to be.

**JC:** To tell you the truth, I don't remember what inspired that one. I remember trying to come up with a "gimmick," and that may very well have been the seed.

**DD:** In a similar vein, is it fair to say that you purposely sought to leverage the popularity of Dungeons & Dragons when you wrote *Hobgoblin*?

**JC:** Oh, definitely. I had a young nephew who was a big D&D guy, and I said to myself "there's got to be a book there." We actually got a letter from the Dungeons & Dragons publishers, saying that we couldn't use the D&D name when promoting the book.

I had a friend of mine, who had a kid who loved the game, and I had him show me how it was played. And then I had to add something different to the mix, so I came up with the Irish mythology idea, which I also knew nothing about before I started researching it. Incidentally, I got more letters about the Hobgoblin than any other book I ever wrote. It just really appealed to kids who were into those kinds of role-playing games at that time.

**DD:** Dover re-published *Hobgoblin* in November of 2015. How did that deal come about, 34 years after the original edition?

**JC:** What happened was, there were all those 15-year-old kids who read the book at that time and loved it, and never forgot about it, even as they grew up and got jobs. And one of them wound up in publishing, and he sought me out to reprint it.

**DD:** Likewise, was *The Shroud* an attempt to capitalize on renewed interest in the Shroud of Turin?

**JC:** Well, there was some renewed interest around that time, but I had been raised as a Roman Catholic, so I always knew about the Shroud, and that it could be a gimmick, very much like stigmata, which I could use in a plot. And I knew enough about the mythology of it to have a running start on writing a book about it.

**DD:** After *The Shroud*, you didn't publish another novel until three years later, in 1986, when you published the mainstream novel, *Brothers and Sisters*. Why such a long break?

**JC:** I was trying to change genres and break into a different area of publishing, and it took a while to write and publish *Brothers and Sisters*. I did publish some short horror stories during that time, but I wasn't writing any horror novels.

**DD:** After that, you returned to horror for three more novels. Let's talk about those three, starting with *The Hunting Season*…

**JC:** Of all my books, I think I like *The Hunting Season* the best. I don't know why, but I do. But I was really starting to run out of steam to write hor-

ror novels. And after *Fury*, I was ready to give up, I couldn't write them anymore.

**DD:** You finished up with *Child of Shadows*. Tell us a little about that book…

**JC:** For that one, I once again set it in remote North Carolina, which I knew from my research for previous books. This woman, the protagonist, takes this child away from the crimes and the evil of New York City down to North Carolina to an artists' community, so that he'll be safe. But she doesn't realize that she's bringing the evil with her, so that's the hook on that one.

After that, I went back to work; I took a full-time job again so I wouldn't have to worry about paying the rent. Then later, on my own, with no contract or anything, I started writing my golf novels.

**DD:** For a male writer, you've used a surprising number of female protagonists. What led to that?

**JC:** You're right… I did use a female protagonist in a lot of my books, but I didn't even think about that until I wrote *The Hunting Season*, and my editor on that one said to me, "for a male, you write female characters very well." So it wasn't purposeful, it just sort of happened that way.

**DD:** You did continue to write some short horror fiction into at least 1993 and '94. Was that solely as a result of receiving invitations to contribute to anthologies, or were you keeping one toe in the water, so to speak, in case the horror genre rebounded?

**JC:** It was more just responding to invites. As I said, I was pretty burned out on horror by that point, at least at novel length.

**DD:** You stated in a 1985 interview with Doug Winter, "…there are a limited number of people who like [horror] novels, and the recent surge

in popularity may have run its course." That statement certainly proved to be prophetic. Do you see any opportunity for the genre to rebound in a big way; to undergo a "boom" period like it did in the '70s and '80s?

**JC:** It actually does seem to me that the occult market is coming back again. I see more evidence of it around, both in terms of books and of movies. It's a lot easier to do movies inexpensively now, and there seems to be a lot of low-budget horror movies being made, which lends to the popularity.

In fact, someone contacted me recently, asking if I'd be interested in making a movie of *The Piercing*? Now, *The Piercing* has floated around forever, on the edge of being made into a movie, but it's never quite happened. But it's possible that it could still happen. The other book that's been optioned, about three times now, is *Hobgoblin*. Those are really the only of my books that have been optioned more than once.

**DD:** Have you considered re-publishing any of your early novels in ebook format?

**JC:** There was an ebook version of *The Piercing* that was published several years ago by NECON. But otherwise there hasn't been any interest.

**DD:** If I'm not mistaken, I believe your website, johncoynebooks.com, received a facelift relatively recently as well. Any particular impetus for that?

**JC:** I wanted to expand it a little bit, and add some stuff on my travel writing. And I also wanted to move over some of the material from my Peace Corps site.

**DD:** Regarding your forthcoming collection… will that contain some unpublished work?

**JC:** Yes, at least three or four of the stories have never been published before. ⬤

THE
DISTANCE
BETWEEN
TWO
POINTS

# BY RJURIK DAVIDSON

"Sorry sight all these loners." The woman smiled wickedly, staring at him with her sapphire-coloured eyes.

They were standing by the window, high up in Colvan's Tower. Outside, permanent seas of dirty air hung like a pall over the industrial planet called Arried. You could never see the stars from anywhere in the city. Around them, the twenty applicants circulated among the institute's coordinators, exchanging pleasant chitchat and discussing the mysterious artifacts brought back from the city on AC-52.

He returned fire. "And yet here *you* are."

"Perhaps I haven't a way with people either."

"No spark." Trence's lips pressed into a half-smile.

"No charm." There was a tinge of laughter in her voice.

"No one who cares." Who *was* this woman?

"The only people who listen to me are fools." She laughed.

On a stage up against a wall, the Supervisor of the institute was projected into the room: a grey man with a grey face who only ever appeared in holograph. Sometimes Trence doubted whether the Supervisor existed at all or was simply a manifestation of the great machine that ran Arried.

There was scattered clapping as the Supervisor surveyed the congregation. "Only three of you will be selected for the journey to AC-52. But those who are chosen—what wonders you will find! An alien city. Among the ruins we will see what mistakes they made, and how we can keep our civilization growing and vibrant, on our pilgrimage across the stars. Dying or dead cultures are always so satisfying, are they not?"

Trence leaned in to the woman. "I'm a pilot, you?"

"Archaeologist. Until now that meant sifting through rubbish on dead worlds. I've worked at the institute for nearly five years. Before that I was a pilot too. Before that, a dancer. From one thing to another, that's me!"

Trence was drawn to her restless energy. "I love to fly. There's nothing that makes you feel quite so alone, out there in the vacuum of space, darkness all around, your wings burning in the cold." The idea of discovery, of seeing something *new*, was a little fire inside him. The mystery of the universe opened him up, the way the sun opens a flower. He'd become a pilot because he wanted to feel the vast weight of space and his miniscule place within it. He needed to see AC-52. He needed to *understand*.

"Alone, huh?" She looked at him curiously. "Come on then."

She grabbed his hand and led him away to the corridors that curled around each other. In a laboratory, small mechanisms lay within clear glass cases. She touched a pad on the side of the display case and took an intricate object into her hand. It looked like a fine lattice butterfly, with the handle in the centre of imbricated wings. It was made of a green and purple material, strong and organic-looking. A strange geometric pattern shifted beneath its surfaces. There was an unnerving impression that the object had more than three dimensions.

"One of the artifacts brought from AC-52. We call this the Connector."

She passed it to him, and it gave a little in his hand. The wings splayed as he held it, and there was a little shudder as something whirred within the mechanism. A charge ran up Trence's arm. Everything went white. Currents reached up through him, connected with the energy fields of the world.

For a moment he was afraid. He thought he might drop the object, but then the truth of things came to him, like shapes emerging from a fog: he could see into the woman, her organs and her bones, her flesh and her blood; he could see her life's energy, pulsing like some immanent promise, radiating into the world. Beyond her

he perceived the internal structures of the walls, the load-bearing sections, the intricate mechanisms of the sliding doors. Farther on rooms and corridors surrounded them, all the way through the Tower and to the spaces beyond, a vast overlapping world.

He knew now that he was but matter in motion, but one element in a complex movement of a greater whole, that he was born, lived, would pass away, but that this was of no greater meaning than the crashing of a wave in a vast ocean. He lost himself, then, and felt himself spread out into those currents that dissolved into the deep structure of the universe; in transcendental bliss he knew that he was Trence no longer, he simply was. Filled with devotion for things, he became aware of the mechanism in his hand closing down again. He was sucked back into himself. He looked up and saw her, and pulled her to him. Their lips met.

Her name was Enmerita, and Trence was afraid.

Enmerita was taken by sudden urges, passions that ignited and were just as quickly snuffed out. In the mornings, they went their separate ways, preparing for the mission. Some afternoons she secreted him away through the Tower, along the wide prospects with their fountains and fake rivers, motorized rickshaws speeding along them, pumping out blackened fumes into the air. The labyrinthine pleasure zone was the busiest section of the Tower. There they passed the exotic kinaesthesia centres, where drugs were combined with exotic forms of massage and tantra. Until finally she would take bring him to the pools, where they would pay for one and loll together, super-oxygenated liquid filling their lungs, and experience exotic ersatz worlds.

In the evenings they ate with the others at the institute, debating humanity's destruction of Arried and the meaning of the city on AC-52. That city! Humanity had crawled over an entire arm of the galaxy, finding life

here and there, but no civilizations, just dumb plants and wild animals, as if evolution had some inbuilt limitation, some ceiling on its development.

Once the archaeologist Xavier shifted his bearlike body in his chair and said, "It's entirely possible that life travelled from planet to planet on asteroids—transpermia."

Lany, slim with mousy hair, let out a soft giggle.

"What?" Xavier's thick eyebrows came together in anger.

Lany burst into an excited jumble of words. "It doesn't mean that evolution would occur in the same way... any intelligent life would be fundamentally different from us."

Xavier shrugged. "We know there's intelligent life, though. The artifacts prove it. And the fact that they affect us shows that whoever built that city must share similar biology."

Enmerita's voice was loud. "Maybe humans jumped planets from Terra long ago and we just don't know about it."

"Terra's dead. We ate it up, just as we're eating this planet up."

"AC-52 proves one thing," said Trence. "We're not alone. Somewhere—perhaps on AC-52 itself, we'll find intelligent life. What will they think, when they see us, and they realize that they are no longer alone either?"

At this, Enmerita looked at the table and her mouth turned down, and Trence suddenly sensed a vast chasm between them. What if only one of them were chosen for the mission? She had hidden depths he would never reach. A quick, liquid anxiety rushed into him.

As the selection date approached, he felt Enmerita slowly withdrawing. Even in the pools she was strangely absent, which made their simulated worlds all the more counterfeit.

One day the Supervisor's hologram appeared in Trence's room, a little too clean-cut, a little too shiny. "You and Xavier and Lany have been chosen for AC-52."

Trence found himself looking out into the brown smog, shuttle burners glowing like embers hidden in the smoke of a fire. He pictured the alien city, but the feeling was now something different: there was a tension there. He put his head in his hands. He thought of Enmerita.

That night she took him out to the mountains. The city sat hidden in a blanket: down there the great mountains of steel and smart matter restlessly growing, throwing grime into the air so that everyone was forced to spend their days in the Towers. Where the sprawling cities ended, the vegetation was stripped, the ground cut open for mining, the seas trawled for the few fish that remained. Soon the populace would leave, migrating *en masse* to the next planet—probably the unspoilt Torion, discovered a decade ago—like locusts towards the nearest field.

But from where they stood, they could see the dazzling stars.

"I'm not going to take the mission," Trence said.

She laughed. "Don't be silly. I'd take it in an instant."

He was silent for a moment. "Don't you want me to stay?"

"It's not that." She laughed again, this time slightly higher and tenser. "It's your dream. You've told me yourself. You want to *understand*."

"From one thing to another, that's you, right?" he said sharply. "But there's an emptiness to that, too, isn't there?"

She turned her head away from him, stood there, looking over the smog that hovered beneath them, a warm and dirty sea. "If it were me, I'd leave you here."

Trence turned quickly, a quick snap and didn't look back. The faster he moved, the less he felt.

Shortly before Trence's departure, Enmerita called him. He ignored her. Later that evening, she arrived outside his room and called through the door. He watched her through the viewer as she looked to her feet, waiting, looked up again, her eyes darting left to the external viewer, in case it lit up with his image. He reached up to activate it, to give her a chance, pulled his hand back slowly, hit the hand-pad clumsily and the door opened.

"I'd like you to stay, if you want to," she said.

"You were right," said Trence. "The universe is out there: a vast array of stars, nebulae, comets cutting across empty space like burning meaning itself. There's a city waiting to speak to us. So, you were right, I'm going."

She stood there, unable to speak, as minute changes turned her face to a taut, white thing.

"Thanks," he nodded slowly. "Thanks."

And so they flew out as a crew of three: Trence, Xavier and Lany.

As the ship blinked in and out of q-space like a flashing light, the three wandered around the tiny passages, floated in the small pools, ate quietly together: Xavier's great bulk hunched over his food like a machine at work, Lany quiet and still, noticing everything.

Sometimes Trence took out the artifacts they carried from AC-52: a thing called the Wire that reached out like a tentacle when you grabbed its handle; the Box, which whirred when pressed at a particular place and made you jump involuntarily, a hundred little shudders one after another; and the Connector, which he never activated. When they arrived on AC-52 they would find the original uses for these objects.

Tension developed between Xavier and Lany. Xavier spoke without looking the slender woman in the eye, as if he was guilty of something. Lany replied in short clipped words. Before long, Trence heard them fucking in the hidden places in the ship. Sometimes he would stand still and listen to their grunting and muffled cries, the little words, "God" and "Please." At other times he ran away and connected with the ship, hanging in the cockpit's harness like a spider in a web, his arms and legs splayed, his head hidden by the helmet. Against his wings, he felt the cold rush of hydrogen plasma, the soft tug of magnetic fields, the brief momentary warmth of radiation.

During the night, Trence woke from nightmares in which he and Enmerita were together again, floating in the pools. "I'm sorry," she would say through the burbling water. Or was it he who said sorry? When he woke, he could never remember. But by now Enmerita would be old or dead. That was how relativity worked; the universe was a place of cold equations.

He felt like a killer.

Not long into the journey, Xavier sat next to Trence in the control room. He spoke in a hesitant voice, as if expecting a sneering reply. "We… we'd like to make a detour, if that's all right with you… Uh, we'd like to see Torion."

"But the mission… the city… you were so passionate about it."

"It just doesn't seem so important now." A small smile played on Xavier's face and he looked back to where Lany stood in the doorway.

Trence knew he should argue the point. Corporate scavengers might strip the city on AC-52 in the decades added by the detour to Torion. But he didn't have the heart for a fight.

Instead, Trence spent more and more time in the pools, enmeshed in fantasies conjured by the computers. He was a dragon slayer riding on an ancient boat; he was a queen in charge of a palace, forcing slaves to pleasure her; he was a sentient spaceship plunging impossibly into black holes. Each time he rose to the pool's surface, the emptiness filled him. There was no reality to any of it. The pools had always been a failed escape.

Fuck it—he wouldn't mind seeing Torion either.

They spun down to Torion like a leaf falling from a tree and Trence was overwhelmed by the great blue of the sea, white and icy at the poles. The continents were small green and grey things. Who could explain that view, its effect on his mind? How could self-generating nature create such wonderful, interlocking systems of wild beauty? For the first time he felt clean, stripped of all the grime of his life.

The ship took them down into the mountains that jagged up like stony knives into the sky. When the door slid up and the stairs uncurled, Trence looked out onto a wide clearing. Grey sponge-like mould ran all the way to a deep-looking river at the base of one of the sheer cliffs.

"Oh." Lany stared at the great craggy peaks looming giddyingly above them. Clouds drifted at terrific speed beyond.

Trence ambled towards a patch of fern-like foliage that rose to about twice his height. The orange plants were little fractal things, each branch sprouted smaller versions of itself. Stooping by a small red plant, he broke off one of its spidery branches. A white milky substance dribbled onto his hand. Dropping it, he reached up to a tree from which hung burgundy-coloured fruit in the shape of a hexagonal prism. He walked through the dappled sunlight to another river, which intersected with the first. Torion was criss-crossed with these rivers, like a great latticework of water running between the mountains.

They slept under the stars that night, and in the morning Xavier fried up pink fish that he caught from the cool waters of the river. As he stirred the fish around in a pan, he looked at the little haven they had found. "Wonderful here—everything you'd need. Water, fish, fruit. You could stay here forever."

"How could there not be intelligent life on one of these planets?" said Trence, who was not yet ready for *that* fight.

Xavier shrugged. "There were, but they destroyed themselves or ran away from their civilization in horror, or transcended the material and became information. Who cares?"

Lany pushed her food around her plate. "Who knows what's at AC-52? Just because scavengers brought back artifacts doesn't mean that it's empty. Scavengers are just machines."

The scavengers who had been unable to penetrate the monstrous city were old automatons, sent decades earlier, designed to find natural resources that might be mined, stripped, consumed.

Trence closed his eyes, felt the sun on his skin, the cool breeze. He dozed for a while, drifting in and out of consciousness, images floating by like little clouds. He felt happy again. Maybe they could stay here, after all.

Afterwards, Xavier and Lany undressed and waded into the cold pool formed in the corner of the wide slow-moving river. Xavier splashed Lany, who laughed and paddled away.

The water was deep and black. The mountains rose at acute angles, so the riverbanks were steep and the river floor hidden far below. A slow movement further out on the river caught Trence's eye, but it was just the shifting of the currents.

"Come on!" Xavier called to Trence.

"Trence! Jump in!" Lany's eyes glistened with life.

Trence unzipped his clothes and ran to the bank. He jumped into the water with a crash, came up for air. "Ah! It's freezing!"

The others laughed and Xavier grabbed Trence by the shoulders and pushed him briefly under. Trence came up again, laughing himself.

"It's not at all like the pools. It's somehow… real." Xavier himself went under for a moment, kicked out. "Hey, what's—"

A tremor ran through Xavier's face, his jaw dropped and his lips opened flaccidly. His eyes darted into a corner and he let out a terrible moan. "My legs! Some—"

Lany screamed and Xavier went underwater again. Trence was instantly aware of the depths of water beneath him. What monsters might lurk down there?

A hand reached out from the water, and Trence lunged forward and grabbed it. He pulled. Instead of Xavier coming up, Trence went under. Lany swam desperately for the shore, crying.

Then Xavier burst through the surface, gasping and crying. A gelatinous thing had engulfed the bottom of his body: something like a giant jellyfish was slithering up him like a translucent sheath. Already, his lower half was being eaten away by some digestive acid, his skin lifting off, revealing the red flesh beneath—

Xavier was being absorbed.

Instinctively, Trence let the hand go and Xavier went under again with a splash.

"No!" Lany leaped back from the bank into the water, splashing towards where Xavier had sunk.

Trence swam towards her. "Lany, he's gone. Lany."

She struck out at him, her face distorted by anger and fear. She was ugly now, moved with the shocking drive of those facing death.

Trence swam for the bank. With each kick he expected his foot to strike something glutinous, something that would glide up over him like wet clothes. But eventually he crawled onto the bank, rolled over onto his elbows. "Lany, come back!"

She reached the spot where Xavier had last been seen and dived into the disturbed waters. Her small white feet the last thing he saw. Slowly weakening concentric circles rippled out. Then everything was still.

That night he sat aboard the ship, stared out at the mountain peaks, dark against the sky. He could return to whatever Arried had become. Perhaps only a skeleton population would be left behind, ageing and dying along with the planet. But the thought depressed him. Instead he would press on to AC-52, to see the ruins. There he might find the secret that eluded him.

As the sunlight broke behind the mountains, he fired the engines and the ship thrust up over Torion. Before long, the grey and green planet dropped away into space, a ball falling into nothingness.

So he came to the fourth planet in star system AC-52, and there descended towards the moon that circled the great gas giant, red and orange above. Great tracts of the moon's red hematite surface had been torn up.

When Trence first saw the mountainous city, some primeval sense overwhelmed him. If Torion awakened the love and fear of nature in him, that structure, like some kind of massive cancerous growth of hexagonal prisms—built by ancient hands—jagged at his mind. Suddenly he perceived the vast tracts of space and time surrounding him. He was an infinitely small point, dissolving.

In the ship's exit chamber, Trence felt the sweat on his back as the suit slid around him and knitted itself together. By the time he stepped from his ship onto the rocky planet, tension weighted his body.

He leaped through the planet's light gravity, the wan green light of the sun hovering in the thin atmosphere, and bounded around the base of the giant conglomeration of hexagonal-shaped structures. Like mammoth spiders' legs, long thin structures emerged from the city, perhaps to hold it steady.

The ship's swarm of beetles spiralled out to survey the place. They informed him that the city was made of the same organic material as the Connector, a flexible organic material stronger than carbon nanotubes.

The swarm found no sign of a door. Trence eventually walked across to the base of one of the spiders' legs. It curved up at a steep angle to the city wall. As he reached out, his arm was pulled suddenly towards the material, as if by magnetic force. A second later, he stepped forward and found himself standing at an acute angle to the ground, as if an alternate gravity emanated from the metal leg and somehow cancelled that of the planet.

He climbed high above the ground until he found himself close to the building's wall, which dilated at his approach. Here was the entrance the scavengers had failed to find.

He continued through the opening, followed by the swarm and sat down quickly. His legs might otherwise have given way from the shock. His mind scampered to make sense of the city. The beetles sped through the air in all directions, sending him readings of distance and temperature, but they had no way of capturing the strangeness of the architecture.

The walkway curved into the structure, intersecting with other walkways that led to the various floors,

walls and roofs. They turned gently as they approached their destinations, so that at times they seemed to be upside down. Each surface seemed to generate its own gravity, so that no matter where one stood, it would feel like walking on the ground.

The swarm informed him that the atmosphere was breathable, and the city a habitable temperature, but Trence kept his helmet fastened.

As he moved along the walkways, he glimpsed dark ruined floors. Where once small structures had stood, now there remained bent pylons and torn and blackened walls. Immense sections of the different floors had been rent by powerful forces. Blackened buildings were scattered around them like dice, their sides were shorn away to reveal clusters of rooms or cells, like bees' nests. On one floor the broken remains of some kind of machine—perhaps a monorail or cable car—lay on its side like a great dead bug.

After about fifteen minutes of walking, bright lights twinkled at him from a faraway plane. Twinkling lights? So out of place in the soft dead light of the city, they called to him like tiny promises of life.

After half an hour of walking, Trence was near enough to see that the lights shone from a seemingly intact floor. Again he was shocked, for there was greenery down there. Life! He wanted to turn and run, to flee this strange fractal city.

Instead, Trence followed the walkway down. An entire garden, lit by lights, was surrounded by buildings, conglomerations of hexagons, like smaller reproductions of the city itself. A garden? Surely that was impossible. He walked past a row of fruit trees, planted in dark earth, and irrigated by a sophisticated system. Beyond the trees he came to a tiny bridge, cobbled together with broken materials from the city. Over the bridge, which spanned a slow moving canal, he stooped by a bed of deep red flowers, which he remembered seeing on Arried.

Trence took off his helmet and breathed the air. It was thin, but pleasant, and the scent of plants drifted to him. He closed his eyes enraptured by this vision, as if someone had projected his dreams in this darkened space.

When he opened his eyes, Trence saw something move. He stood quickly, his heart beating rapidly. One of the trees close to him shifted.

Something was stalking him.

"Trence," a voice said. "Trence, close your eyes again."

Panic gripped him, for the creature knew his name. He could vaguely make the figure out hidden behind the tree and some madness overtook him. Something was profoundly wrong. Was his feverish mind collapsing in upon itself, projecting its fantasies, or was this alien city some nightmare zone?

"Who are you?" he said.

The figure stepped from behind the tree.

Trence stared, his mind refusing to register the image. But there was something discordant about her. He thought it was Enmerita, but she was too old. Lines creased the side of her face, and her fiery hair was shot with silver. Her face had widened, her body gently sagged. Now she was in her fifties, perhaps.

She looked away, embarrassed, then back to him. "Trence, it's me."

He stood there dumb, before his mind jumped into action again: he was hallucinating. Or she was some kind of vision constructed by the city, an illusion, a siren sent to ruin him.

She reached out to him, but he pushed her away.

She stepped back. "Why did you take so long?"

"Get away from me, whatever you are."

"Please." Again she reached out.

This time he shoved her powerfully and she fell, putting her arms behind her to break her fall. A look of pain crossed her face and she looked at her left wrist. She pulled herself to her feet—the action of a woman who had lost her sprightliness.

"Trence," There was doubt in her voice: a voice that sounded just like Enmerita. She took a step towards him and he took a several steps backwards.

Tears filled her eyes, she turned and ran from him, silver and scarlet hair bouncing on her back.

Trence returned to the garden and passed among the fruit trees. There were oranges, and yes, definitely heli-fruit from Arried. There were yellow grapes and small patches of a green grain he didn't recognize. It was the kind of collection that most exploratory ships carried. A terrible possibility struggled to assert itself at the edges of his mind.

The hexagonal building appeared at the end of the row, a miniature reproduction of the city-chamber it resided in. Behind it sat an exploratory ship, just like the one he had arrived in.

There seemed to be no entrance to the building, but when he came near an aperture dilated open. Stepping inside, he was taken aback by the bright starlight that gleamed down on him: the planes of the roof pictured the night sky. The room was littered with intricately patterned cushions and mats, while incense hovered in the air—just as Enmerita would have designed.

He found her lying on a collection of multicoloured blankets. On the wall behind her hung a great collection of earrings: some bands, others dangling long and low. There was a sinking in Trence's chest.

She looked up at him. "It was a shock when I arrived and you weren't here. At first it was moment by moment—I expected you to arrive any day. And then after a few months, I thought about going back. But I thought, 'What am I going back to?' The plans to migrate to Torion are already underway. And I thought: no, I'd prefer to stay here."

"You're not real." He said. "You're a construction of this city."

"I followed you. I was wrong, see. I knew it at the time, but I found myself doing the same thing. Running, as I always do. 'From one thing to another' I used to say. That's the irony of life. We know we're making the same mistakes, but we make them again and again. You did the same thing too, didn't you? That wasn't the first time you chose to be alone."

"Damn you! What have you done to us? You're an old woman." Relativity had worked its equations on them.

"You turned me away. What did *you* do to us?"

He put his head in his hands and then found himself next to her, kneeling, and she embracing him, and he felt the ginger and silver hair against his cheek and he clutched her and felt the thickness that had crept into her body with age. "Damn you, me… Damn."

Later, after the halting, agonizing first words, the slow struggle from awkwardness, the recriminations and reconciliations, the slow settling of the truth, Enmerita looked from where she sat among a sea of cushions. "I've searched through the city. There are all kinds of technology, all kinds of instruments and mechanisms whose use I couldn't decipher. But no sign of life. There is one place, though, at the centre of the city… Perhaps some kind of control room, but it's eerie. When I first visited it, I found it too strange. With each day I put it off, just as I put off returning to Arried, until it all seemed too late. I was trapped here… stasis, I suppose. Fear of everything else."

He rolled from the floor into a squat. "It's time don't you think? Are you ready to find out?"

"I'll come with you but I'll just watch," she said.

They prepared themselves and crossed the city, moving from one blackened and blasted surface to another. Pieces of machinery lay strewn around the floors, mechanisms that whirred and hummed, others as intricate as latticework.

Trence found his eyes drawn again and again to Enmerita. She was different. It wasn't just the weight she carried or the streaks of grey in her hair. The years spent alone had made her introspective. Her fiery passion was softened by a newfound contemplative nature. His anger still burned and confused him: she was in her fifties now—twenty years older than him—and there was nothing that could be done about that.

At the centre of the vast hall, twisting walkways joined together at a hexagon-shaped building about the size of a house. Enmerita touched a pad and an aperture dilated before them.

Inside, green and purple geometric patterns hovered just above the surface of the chamber's walls—a hundred moving holograms. There was something odd to those patterns and shapes: rich and detailed triangles and quadrilaterals whose angles seemed wider than was possible, giving a sense that they were somehow refracted by the space around them.

For a while they examined what appeared to be screens of some sort, hanging on the walls. But no matter how they touched them, nothing

> He found her lying on a collection of multicoloured blankets. On the wall behind her hung a great collection of earrings: some bands, others dangling long and low. There was a sinking in Trence's chest.

occurred. Finally, they sat down in silence and looked up at a bowl-like object—it might have been a seat, smooth and black—hovering in the air above them.

Something lurked in the back of Trence's mind, struggling to emerge. He lifted his head sharply. "The Connector."

Trence took the mechanism from his pack: the patterns on its surfaces mirrored those of the room. The imbricated wings opened. Energy coursed into Trence, warm and beautiful, and the deep structures of the world unveiled themselves to him: Enmerita's body, its organs and bones; the arrangement of metal, shimmering with energy; and above him the seat, powered by some ancient technology. He reached up to it with his mind, coursing into it even as he lost himself, just a transcendent wave amongst the many others. The seat shuddered into action. Humming softly, it began to descend. Trence sucked himself back, and the Connector closed. He took a step backwards and a moment later the chair shuddered to a stop before him.

Without further thought, Trence lurched into the seat. Slowly it began to rise again, like some kind of throne. Through the skin of his arms, he could feel warmth. To his horror, his hands had been encased by the seat's black material: some kind of viscous metal or plastic that slid over him.

His body jolted, as if from an electric shock. He felt a stabbing pain. His mind jagged once more. Then he became aware of the city's walls and its apertures, of a million little networks of environment controls, the way it moved liquids and energy, q-bits like protective white blood cells. He dissolved further into the system, like a river into the sea. As he lost sense of himself, he became aware not only of the physicality of the city, but its history too, and he found himself watching those creatures.

They came to AC-52 in some vast and irregular ship, a dark thing, its colours the familiar intermixed green and purple. There was a bizarre aspect to the vessel, but Trence was engrossed by the creatures themselves, things that shambled and crawled on the planet's surface. Each was the size of Enmerita's hexagonal house. They resembled squat caterpillars with odd protuberances from their purplish bodies, which rolled and extended as they crawled. They had no eyes, but could sense topography though some other method. A strange gleam came from their bodies, a dark sickly light.

He watched them construct the city with their weird organic machines. He saw the complex methods they used to distract themselves from the meaning of their activity. He watched them bustle around the floors of the city, so busy and industrious. They held strange rituals of communication, where they could roll and join in a great seething and curling mass. One of the creatures sat in the very seat that Trence occupied, and monitored the city and its populace.

Trence found he could enter the creature's mind, and he felt a terrible, sharpness behind his eyes. Now he saw the secret of their strange dark light. They moved in multiple dimensions, bulging into the three familiar ones, retreating into others. Trence's mind was pulled in strange ways. It was discomposed, cracked at the edges. Some part of him felt his hands clenched madly in the chair. He tried to cry, but he could not. He was human, a species that thought and moved through time in three dimensions. How could he understand those creatures' thoughts, their motions and desires?

And so for some unknown reason they warred, burning and breaking their own city, and then retreated from the planet, not away in space, but away from the universe itself. The creature rolled from the seat and its mind pulled away from Trence, like a gas dissipating into space. Trence's psyche recomposed itself. He watched the creature stretch its way into a ship, which not so much flew but disappeared.

When he came to, he heard the sound of Enmerita calling up to where he sat. Somehow he brought the seat to ground and the seat released him. He staggered out, senseless, speechless.

"You saw something terrible, didn't you?"

"No," he said. "I don't know what I saw. It wasn't terrible. Well, it was, but only because… I didn't understand. We came all this way to find something incomprehensible, something—" Finally he settled on a word. "Alien."

When they returned to Enmerita's building it was late. There they lay in the central room, staring at the unfamiliar constellations on the ceiling. In the starlight, the wrinkles beneath Enmerita's eyes had softened. He reached out and ran his thumb over them. Despite her age, her eyes were still large and wonderfully blue.

"What do you make of it? Of these creatures, this city?" said Enmerita.

Trence tried to capture his thoughts. To convey them was to express the mind of the alien. Words could only ever be an approximation. Even now he felt decentred.

"They weren't us," he said. "They will never be us."

"But what does that mean?" she said.

"I don't know," he said. "There's no humanity here. I thought that we would meet intelligent life and we would communicate with it. Now I… it's a mystery. Of course they're not us. We're still alone."

"But we are here, you and I. Humanity *is* here."

"I suppose that's true. I travelled all this way, to find not an alien species— but you," said Trence.

She slid over and wrapped her arms around him. "We would have had beautiful children."

"It's too late now."

Enmerita's head was warm against Trence's shoulder, and her hair rested lightly against his face.

"I'll die before you," she said sadly.

"You will." He pressed his face into her hair. "But not yet. Not yet."

Enmerita reached over and took his hand in hers and together they looked up through the transparent roof to the stars, twinkling out in the black sky with the promise of life. ◗

# TheHieroglyphs of Blood and Bone
## Visionary new voice in weird fiction Michael Griffin

When Guy's marriage of two decades unravels, he's driven from his previously stable domestic life and ends up renting a room in the houseboat of his much younger co-worker Karl. Pushed outside his comfort zone, Guy tries to follow Karl's example, until he ends up exploring entirely new frontiers, both natural and uncanny.

He finally encounters the enigmatic Lily, who offers to share with Guy her own arcane language, a mix of incomprehensible symbols, rough bits of nature and dark pleasures of the flesh. Guy finds himself obsessed, as if powerless under Lily's spell.

Will he recognize in time the many secrets she keeps hidden in plain sight, or will allow himself to be pulled downstream toward an inescapable vortex?

### Publication Date: February 24, 2017

# Wind Through the Fence
## And Other Stories

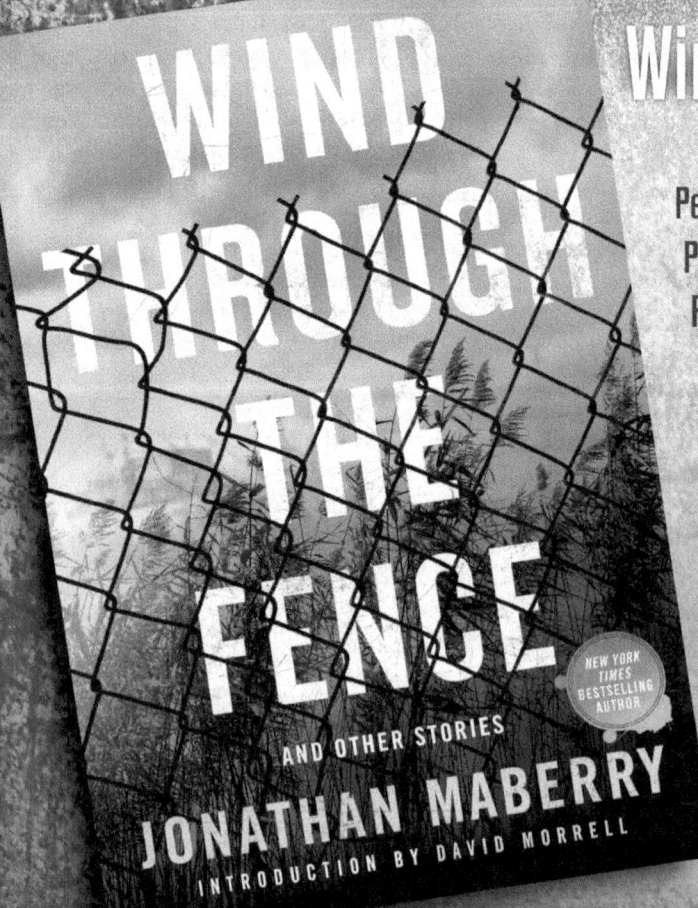

Pegleg and Paddy Save the World

Plan 7 from L.A.

Red Dreams

Saint John

She's Got a Ticket to Ride

Spellcaster 2.0

T. Rhymer – Written with Gregory Frost

The Cobbler of Oz

The Things That Live in Cages

The Vanishing Assassin

The Wind through the Fence

Faces

### Publication Date: February 10, 2017